It had been the worst afternoon of Sam Miller's life...

...until now. Things were suddenly looking up. He'd been watching the members of the Whipple gang from across the street, never dreaming that such a spectacular woman was just inside. He watched her lift a graceful hand to sweep back her pale hair in a gesture so feminine and so unconsciously sensual that it made his ears smoke.

Her eyes met his.

Rockets shot through him. He forgot about the Whipples, the stolen ring—forgot everything but her. He had to meet her. He moved toward the door. The woman also took a step, and that was when Sam saw the jewels. His mouth dropped open. He couldn't believe his eyes, but the evidence was in plain sight!

Dear Reader,

Welcome to Silhouette—experience the magic of the wonderful world where two people fall in love. Meet heroines who will make you cheer for their happiness, and heroes (be they the boy next door or a handsome, mysterious stranger) who will win your heart. Silhouette Romance reflects the magic of love—sweeping you away with books that will make you laugh and cry, heartwarming, poignant stories that will move you time and time again.

In the coming months we're publishing romances by many of your all-time favorites, such as Diana Palmer, Brittany Young, Sondra Stanford and Annette Broadrick. Your response to these authors and our other Silhouette Romance authors has served as a touchstone for us, and we're pleased to bring you more books with Silhouette's distinctive medley of charm, wit and—above all—*romance*.

I hope you enjoy this book and the many stories to come. Experience the magic!

Sincerely,

Tara Hughes
Senior Editor
Silhouette Books

BEVERLY TERRY

Thief of Hearts

Silhouette *Romance*

Published by Silhouette Books New York

America's Publisher of Contemporary Romance

To Mari Veneziano
and her love of Miami

 SILHOUETTE BOOKS
300 E. 42nd St., New York, N.Y. 10017

Copyright © 1989 by Beverly Haaf

ISBN: 0-373-08685-7

First Silhouette Books printing November 1989

All the characters in this book are fictitious. Any
resemblance to actual persons, living or dead, is
purely coincidental.

®: Trademark used under license and
registered in the United States Patent and
Trademark Office and in other countries.

Printed in the U.S.A.

Books by Beverly Terry

Silhouette Romance

Before the Loving #414
The Love Bandit #607
Thief of Hearts #685

BEVERLY TERRY

lives in New Jersey. She and her husband met while in college, and she taught elementary school before staying home to raise a family. Although she has written magazine features and newspaper articles on a variety of subjects, her main love has always been fiction writing—mysteries, the occult and, of course, romance. She also enjoys doing portrait painting, but she says that her painting is fictional, too, as the portraits rarely turn out to look like the real person.

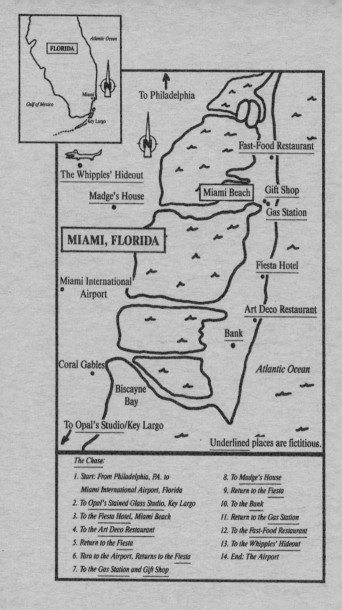

FLORIDA

Atlantic Ocean

Gulf of Mexico

Miami

Key Largo

To Philadelphia

Fast-Food Restaurant

The Whipples' Hideout

Madge's House

Miami Beach

Gift Shop

Gas Station

MIAMI, FLORIDA

Fiesta Hotel

Miami International
Airport

Art Deco Restaurant

Bank

Coral Gables

Atlantic Ocean

Biscayne
Bay

To Opal's Studio/Key Largo

Underlined places are fictitious.

The Chase:

*1. Start: From Philadelphia, PA. to
   Miami International Airport, Florida*

2. To Opal's Stained Glass Studio, Key Largo

3. To the Fiesta Hotel, Miami Beach

4. To the Art Deco Restaurant

5. Return to the Fiesta

6. Tara to the Airport, Returns to the Fiesta

7. To the Gas Station and Gift Shop

8. To Madge's House

9. Return to the Fiesta

10. To the Bank

11. Return to the Gas Station

12. To the Fast-Food Restaurant

13. To the Whipples' Hideout

14. End: The Airport

Chapter One

W ell, now," Tara Linton said to herself as she saw the good-looking, stylishly dressed man heading her way along the blustery Philadelphia street. "Wouldn't I like to pack him in my Florida vacation bag!"

She watched him stride like a man with urgent matters on his mind, his expression intent as he blindly passed by her and hurried on. She pulled the collar of her pale blue designer coat up against the sharp November wind and turned to stare after him. Fascinated, she kept her eyes on his retreating back until he turned the corner.

Half an hour later, her errands completed, Tara found herself glancing about for the stranger as she retraced her steps. He was nowhere around, of course. Amused at her foolishness, she opened the door to Randalls' Decorating Showroom, hearing the pleasant jingle of the bell. As always, the snug shop, with its crowded displays of antiques and museum-quality reproductions, filled her with pride. The business dealt mostly with decorators, but during her

four years there, Tara had encouraged walk-in trade and the
profits had increased. She'd worked her way up to manager
and planned to eventually buy out the owner, who was already semi-retired.

As she closed the door, she noticed two sandy-haired men
looking at the unicorn tapestries. Something in their manner made Tara think they would feel more at home with
bowling trophies on their mantel instead of art treasures—
but that didn't mean they didn't have money to burn. Slipping off her coat, she was about to approach them when
Annette, her assistant, called her to the desk in the showroom's corner.

"I took an order for the other jade dragon," Annette
announced with a grin. Twenty-two years old to Tara's
twenty-five, she was dark-haired and pixieish. "Mrs. Stern
bought it for her penthouse garden."

"Oh, Annette—wonderful!" Tara beamed. There had
been a time when one such expensive sale in a month would
have been a royal coup, and now this made two in a week.
With Annette in charge, Tara knew she needn't worry while
she was away on vacation. Smiling to herself, she hung up
her coat and turned to the carton sitting on the chair.

"Are these the stained glass materials we're shipping
ahead to Opal Carson in Florida?"

"Yes, I've already called the parcel service, but—" Annette cast a glance at the two men, who still seemed absorbed in the tapestries "—I left the top open because I
figured you'd add the gem-cuts. Or are you taking them
with you?"

"No, I have enough to pack and carry already." Still
talking, Tara opened her tote bag and pulled out the small
plastic bag of gem-cut glass she'd picked up at the stained
glass supply house. "Boy, is this tote stuffed. I stopped at
the travel agent's for my tickets and she loaded me up with

folders. Plus, I've got a nice fat novel for the beach." She shook her head. "You know, I still can't believe I'm lucky enough to have a client foot the bill for a week in Miami. All I have to do for it is run down to the Keys and meet with Opal Carson—and that's going to be fun!"

"That's the spirit," Annette said approvingly. "It's your first real vacation in almost two years, so let yourself go. I bet those Florida beaches are crawling with wild, fun-loving guys."

Tara shrugged, not bothering to say that wasn't the kind of vacation she wanted. Dating for laughs had no appeal. After growing up with three wonderful but wacky big brothers, she'd had it up to here with "fun-loving" guys. She was sick of men whose notion of style was an apology after burping at will. Thoughts of the well-dressed stranger she'd noticed on the street went through her mind. With someone like him, birthdays would mean French restaurants and ballet tickets, not Burger King with a whoopee cushion under her chair and a gag gift of anatomically correct boy and girl pot holders. So what if Annette thought she was a fussy stick-in-the-mud? She was busy building a career, and if a man wasn't a romantic "Mr. Right," why waste the effort?

She glanced at her watch. "Isn't it time for your lunch?"

A guarded expression slipped over Annette's face. She leaned forward and whispered, "I'm staying until that pair leave."

"Oh?" Tara looked more closely at the men, who had moved to examine a Chinese screen. They were medium height and medium-boned, one slightly chunkier than the other. The set of their eyes and same hair color made them look alike, except that one had a pinched face and a fretful expression, while the chunky one, busy chewing gum, simply looked bored. They appeared harmless enough.

"They acted jumpy when they first came in," Annette continued softly. "They claimed they wanted to browse for a present for an aunt. But it sounded fishy. Maybe they're up to something."

Tara narrowed her eyes. When it came to her shop, she wanted to know the score. "Let's see what they tell me," she decided without hesitation, stepping toward them.

Close up, she thought they appeared even more harmless. "I'm Tara Linton, the manager," she said pleasantly. "My assistant tells me you're looking for a gift?"

"Ah, yeah," the chunky man mumbled, shifting his gum to the other side of his mouth. He smelled like spearmint. "For our sister."

"Our aunt," his companion corrected, poking him with an elbow. "It's our aunt, Moss. Our aunt."

"Oh, yeah, that's right, Elmo." Moss nodded slowly. "Our aunt needs a present, too. They both need presents."

Fishy is right, Tara thought. Aloud, she said, "I noticed you admiring the tapestries."

"They're too big," Elmo answered with a frown. "Our aunt hasn't got much wall space."

"Her apartment is real little," Moss contributed. After a thoughtful chew on his gum, he added, "Our sister's apartment is little, too."

Tara found herself curious enough to play along. Leading them back to the tapestries, she realized she still carried the little plastic bag of cut glass. She switched it to her left hand so she could gesture with her right.

"I'm sure you've already noticed that these are composed of one large scene surrounded by smaller ones." She bent forward as she talked, a curving wing of her short, wheat-blond hair swinging across her cheek. "You might consider ordering handmade reproductions of a smaller scene."

"Sounds good." Elmo gave a glance toward the window, then stepped behind a tapestry and knelt to peer fretfully at a small scene near the bottom. Tara decided his worried expression was habitual.

Moss moved to squat beside him. "Which one are we looking at, Elmo?"

A movement out on the sidewalk caught Tara's eye. Smoothing back her hair, she turned toward the window. Her heart leaped.

The stranger was crossing the street and coming toward the shop. A chill shivered up Tara's spine. It seemed a stroke of fate to have him show up again. He paused in front of the glass and peered inside. Tara couldn't stop staring. His smoothly cut hair was a rich sable brown and something in the expression on his lean, handsome face struck her, as it had on the street, as provocatively mysterious. Everything about his appearance was up-to-date perfection, his unbuttoned top coat impeccably cut, his necktie a stylish pattern.

Was he coming inside? She tried to get a grip on herself. She was acting like a love-struck schoolgirl. Okay, so he looked absolutely gorgeous, but there was no way he could be as perfect as he appeared.

Elmo looked up from his crouched position. "I heard you talk about flying tomorrow to Miami and the Keys. Nice vacation spot."

"Yes. Thank you." Her reply was distracted. She tried to focus on her customer, but her attention was drawn back to the window. The stranger matched her fantasy "Mr. Right" so exactly it was almost a sin. He was simply too good to be true. She saw him move toward the door and took an unconscious step in his direction. He was coming in. There had to be something wrong with him, didn't there? At the very least, he would turn out to be married.

* * *

It had been the worst afternoon of Sam Miller's life—
until now. But things were suddenly looking up. He'd been
freezing his tail off, keeping watch on two of the three
members of the Whipple gang from across the street, never
dreaming that such a spectacular woman was inside. She
must have entered when he'd run to see if the boy who'd
fallen from his bike was hurt. The boy had been okay, but
when Sam moved back to where he'd been keeping watch on
the showroom, the Whipples were no longer in sight. He'd
crossed the street for a closer look and confirmed his fears—
Elmo and Moss Whipple were gone. He'd felt cold, disgusted and miserable until a glimpse of the stunner inside
warmed him all over. Or at least warmed him until he again
remembered he'd lost his quarry.

The only redeeming factor was that he had an excuse to
go into the shop and meet the breathtaking blonde. He
could question her about the Whipples, then edge into other
topics, like dinner, dancing and eggs Benedict for breakfast. She was tall and lithe, with full hips, a slim waist and
high, rounded breasts. He watched her lift a graceful hand
to sweep back her pale hair in a gesture so feminine and unconsciously sensual that it made his ears smoke.

Her eyes met his.

Rockets shot through him. He forgot about the Whipples—forgot everything but her. He had to meet her. He
moved toward the door. The woman also took a step, and
that was when Sam saw the jewels. His mouth dropped
open. He couldn't believe his eyes, but the evidence was in
plain sight. He shook his head in stunned realization. She
had to be in cahoots with Elmo and Moss Whipple, and the
unset gems she carried as casually as a bag of jelly beans
were part of the stash lifted from the Dwight-Astor safe. He
understood now—the Whipples hadn't ducked into the

showroom to hide, they'd come to make a delivery. In a state of shock, Sam realized he was no longer entering the showroom to question an innocent woman. He was going in to meet the fence for a robbery gang.

Almost painfully aware of the handsome stranger who'd just entered, Tara's thoughts went to her appearance. She hurried to the mirror behind the desk, dropping the bag of glass stones into the open carton as she bent to peer at her reflection. If only she'd worn a different dress, something more flattering, a better color. Too late now. She straightened. *Be calm. Think poise. It's now or never.* She pivoted to face the stranger, a welcoming smile ready on her lips.

An alarmed shout from Moss interrupted the moment.

"Hey, Elmo!"

Tara turned to see the two men popping up from behind the tapestries like jack-in-the-boxes.

Everything exploded into action.

Elmo stumbled over a rolled-up Turkish rug on his way to one side of the shop, while Moss took off in the opposite direction. The handsome stranger shouted something and went after him, knocking over the pony from a Victorian carousel in the process. The falling pony set Indian brasses bouncing against Art Deco chrome. Tara rushed toward the commotion as the stranger succeeded in grabbing Moss. Their struggles tipped over a shelf of porcelain cups and saucers. Moss shoved the stranger against the Egyptian display and tumbled him to the floor.

"The cat!" screamed Annette.

Tara saw an Egyptian pottery cat statue, an expensive reproduction of a tomb treasure, rock wildly on its pedestal. The stranger, sprawled on his back, lay groaning on the floor at its base. Moss trampled across him as he galloped to the door. Elmo darted from the opposite direction and followed out on Moss's heels.

The door slammed behind them.

The Egyptian statue toppled and fell.

Tara rushed forward but couldn't get there in time.

The stranger looked up. He saw the statue coming and lifted his arms. "Ooough!" The heavy, four-foot-high clay cat thunked safely against his chest and stomach.

Clothes no longer impeccable, his hair tumbling across his forehead, he lay clutching the pottery treasure. He looked up plaintively from Annette to Tara.

"Meow?" he said.

Tara couldn't believe her ears.

Meow?

Annette giggled, but all Tara could think was that the inanity was something her brothers might say. Buddy, Bobby or Cal . . . any one of them would be capable of it. But not her hero. In this sort of situation, the man she'd dreamed of would respond with—Wait just a darned minute. She shook her head. Her hero would never *be* in such a situation.

In shock, she stared around the showroom. A disaster. The average train wreck was probably neater. Knocked-over canvases, tilted shelves, precious objets d'art strewn like so much flotsam and jetsam . . . She started to tremble as reaction set in. At least the Egyptian cat was safe, and that had been the most expensive item in the showroom. And the man who had saved it lay almost at her feet.

Despite her earlier thoughts, he was her hero, and he was hurt. She hurried forward and dropped to her knees beside him. How could she have thought of criticizing him? The poor man had probably spoken in a delirium. He'd been knocked down, trampled, and a fifty-pound chunk of statuary had nearly squashed him flat. No wonder he'd babbled nonsense.

"Are you all right?" she cried.

He looked at her, revealing eyes that were a beautiful cinnamon shade. He groaned.

"Goodness!" Tara cried. "You can hardly breathe. Here, let me move this statue." Her kneeling position made it difficult to lift the pottery cat, which was even heavier than she remembered. Annette moved to help.

"He's awfully cute," Annette whispered into Tara's ear as they hefted the cat. She giggled. "And it's obvious he's fallen for you."

"Please," Tara chided, irritated that Annette would joke at such a time. She returned her attention to the stranger. "How do you feel? Are you injured?"

Sam marveled over the sincere, caring note in her voice. She didn't sound like a person mixed up in crime. The brunette had called her Tara. Groaning, he started to get up.

"Here," she said, putting an arm around his shoulder and leaning toward him. "Let me help."

Sam's head spun. He didn't know if his dizziness was a reaction to the blonde's warm nearness, getting squashed by the statue or a combination of both. He allowed himself to slump forward, his head coming to rest against her breasts.

Cradled in her arms, he heard her say, "Oh, gosh, Annette—he's blacked out!" *Not really,* he argued silently. He felt a lot better than he was acting. He needed time to think—except that the lushness pillowing his cheek made it difficult to keep his thoughts in place.

He groaned again, and this time the source of his ache was far from a couple of bruised ribs. Tara. It was an elegant, regal name, like tiara. It suited her perfectly. How could she be dealing with creeps like the Whipples? He supposed he should be philosophic about the situation. Whatever she was, she was. And one of the things she was, was a woman who put perfume between her breasts. Its scent was wonderful—a crisp, refined fragrance that made him think

of classic pearls, white gloves and champagne, but then it
gave way to an undernote that was so incredibly sensual
that—

Sam, he ordered himself sharply. *Get your thoughts back
to business.* And business, in this case, was locating a piece
of jewelry lifted from the Dwight-Astor safe—the Bonbon
Ring.

The Bonbon, a ring with a bonbon-shaped ruby, had
supposedly once belonged to Queen Isabella of Spain. Mrs.
Dwight-Astor had worn the Bonbon to a party and her
husband, Freddy, was supposed to have returned it to the
bank vault with the rest of her jewels. Instead, he'd put it in
the mansion safe and forgot about it until the robbery. The
ransacked safe had been stuffed with goodies, but the only
thing Freddy was desperate to recover was the ring—and he
wanted it back without his wife's ever learning it had been
missing.

Freddy, who was a friend of Sam's father, told Sam he
would pay big for the Bonbon's return, no questions asked.
If Sam, a junior account executive for an insurance firm,
successfully regained the ring, the business for the entire
Dwight-Astor Chemical Corporation would be added to
Freddy's personal property coverage that Sam already had
in his portfolio. Accepting the challenge, Sam had learned
that a trio of crooked cousins, known as the Whipple gang,
had pulled the robbery, but now that he'd so deliciously
made the acquaintance of their fence, he no longer needed
them. All he needed was the help of this exquisite female
cradling him like a motherless child. He heard Annette say,
"I'll call the police and an ambulance."

Not needing a doctor, Sam reluctantly lifted his head from
Tara's breast. "No, I'm okay. Really." He blinked, trying
to keep his recovery from seeming too miraculous. "I'm
fine."

"Are you sure?" Tara asked.

"Yes, I'm sure." Accepting her help, he got up. He brushed off his clothes, his thoughts racing. Elmo and Moss were under the impression he was a cop—they might have told her the law was after them. If she realized he was the one they meant, she would be scared off before he could explain his mission. The more he considered her manner, the more convinced he became that he'd been wrong in thinking she was an experienced professional. Maybe she didn't even understand that a crime had been committed. Maybe this was something she thought of as a lark. She would be terrified if she believed he was the law. He needed to gain her confidence. For starters, he would play the part of an innocent bystander.

"Are you sure you're all right?" Tara asked.

"I'm positive." He smiled down at her. "The wind was just knocked out of me."

"I knew those two guys were bad news," Annette said. "What made you go after them?"

Thinking fast, Sam explained, "They acted so suspicious and when the one guy ran, I thought I'd better try to stop him. After that, I'm not sure what happened."

"What happened was that you saved a costly reproduction," Tara said gratefully. "I can't tell you how thankful we are."

Liking the idea of her gratitude, he looked around. "This place has really been trashed." Inspiration struck. "This is when you need really good advice about your insurance claim."

"I hadn't thought about insurance." Tara's expression was worried. "I hope our policy covers situations like this."

"I'm sure it does," he soothed. "But the paperwork can be confusing. I know. Insurance is my game." He handed her his card. Now she would see he wasn't a cop.

She looked at the card, which said he was with Super State Insurance. "This isn't the company we're with."

Sam thought she sounded disappointed, which he took as an encouraging sign. "It doesn't matter. You probably have a standard policy. Not that you couldn't eventually figure it out for yourself, but I probably know a few shortcuts that will help speed up your claim." All he had to do now was get her away from the brunette, who might not be in on the jewel deal. Then he would lose no time explaining that any big money wouldn't come from insurance—it would come from Freddy Dwight-Astor as soon as she turned over the Bonbon Ring.

"I feel involved and I'd really like to help. Suppose we study your policy over a cup of coffee. We'll see what we can do to get all this damage taken care of." He looked at her as he talked, thinking he could gaze into her beautiful gray eyes forever.

"Oh, that would be wonderful—" Tara's enthusiasm sputtered to a halt. "My trip!" She put her hands to her face. "With all this mess, I can't just take off for Miami."

Miami? Sam was electrified. Of course! She wasn't a crook at all. She'd been conned into thinking she was doing someone a favor on her trip. In Miami, she would pass the stuff to a contact who would whisk it out of the country. But she wouldn't realize that. The idea that the goods were stolen would come as a total shock.

"You're a nut if you cancel because of this," Annette said. She waved a hand around the showroom. "This is a clean-up problem, not a major disaster. When the police arrive, we'll make a report and then you just go home early and finish packing, exactly as planned. I can itemize the damage and get things cleaned up. If you'd already left, I'd be the one in charge, right?"

The bell jingled as a uniformed messenger from the parcel service entered. "Wait by the desk," Annette told him. "I'll have the package sealed and ready in a second." Turning, she gave Tara a parting shot. "You're the boss—you can do what you want, but in my opinion it's ridiculous to even think of giving up your vacation."

"I guess she's right," Tara said to Sam as Annette left to attend to the messenger.

"She probably is," he agreed. He was now thoroughly convinced that Tara didn't realize what she was mixed up in. She was a maiden in distress and didn't even know it. It was his duty to rescue her.

In the background, the phone rang. "It's for you, Tara," the brunette called.

Tara gave Sam a warm look. "If you'll excuse me a moment?"

On her way to the phone, Tara felt as if she walked on air. She glanced down at his card again. Sam Miller, Account Executive. What a man! Like a knight on a white horse, his first act upon entering her life had been to perform a heroic deed. The fact that he was so willing to help her get the best possible insurance settlement didn't tarnish his armor, either. He really seemed awfully nice.

Reaching the desk, she stepped to one side so the parcel service messenger, carton in his arms, could get by.

"It's Opal Carson," Annette whispered, one hand cupped over the mouthpiece.

Wondering why she would be calling, Tara reached for the phone. Opal Carson was the stained glass artist she'd found to create a series of stained glass panels for Gary and Greta Hazelton's new home. Opal had agreed to work from plans that would be mailed to her, but the wealthy Hazeltons had decided they wanted Tara to discuss the specifications in person, which was how the all-expenses-paid trip had come about.

"Hello, Mrs. Carson," she said. "How can I help you?"

"You can help by remembering that it's Opal, just Opal. You'll make me feel older than seventy, which is ancient enough."

"All right, Opal." Tara laughed, liking the woman, who she'd previously known only through letters. "Now, how can I help you?"

As she talked, she glanced across the showroom at Sam, who was moving to open the door for the messenger. He caught her look and his smile sent tingles running along her skin.

Basking in the glow of Tara's gaze, Sam helped the parcel service man out and was about to close the door when he saw Moss Whipple driving down the street. He groaned inwardly. He should have guessed. The Whipples were hanging around, protecting their interests. But where was Elmo?

He shot a worried look toward Tara, who talked on the phone. Suppose Elmo was on the other end? Nervously, he imagined Elmo telling her something bad about him to scare her off. Then, when he tried to explain to her that she was mixed up in a robbery, she wouldn't believe him. She would probably even say he'd imagined the bag of unset stones.

Sam wondered where she'd put the stones. They'd been in her hand just before he'd jumped Moss. With all the commotion, she might have simply set them down. She couldn't deny her involvement if he could find them. Stepping around broken crystal, he moved toward the tapestries, the place where he'd last seen her with the gems. It put him close enough to overhear her talking to someone she called Opal. He eavesdropped shamelessly, knowing it was for a good cause.

"There was a delay because I couldn't get the last item until this afternoon, but a messenger just took the carton to the airport. It's a rush order shipment, so it may even reach you before I do."

Sam froze. She was talking about sending stuff to Miami. Damn, what a dunce he'd been. She'd put the stones in the carton—the carton that had been carried out almost under his nose. He'd even held the door! He wanted to kick himself. The Bonbon Ring was probably in the package, too. It was out of his grasp now. Maybe even gone for good.

He clenched his fists, feeling helpless and thoroughly frustrated. He was a top-notch insurance man, but he sure as hell wasn't a secret agent.

Chapter Two

On a jet flying south the following morning, Tara sat by the window, her tote and overnight bag on the empty seat next to her. Resting her head back, she reviewed for the hundredth time what had happened the previous afternoon after she'd finished speaking with Opal Carson and had turned to face Sam Miller.

"Ah, look, I...I've got to go," he'd told her. He'd pointed to his watch. "I...I just realized I'm almost late. Uh, for an appointment."

Startled by his obvious eagerness to leave, she'd said, "But the police will probably have some questions."

"Then give them my card and they can reach me, okay?"

She hardly had time to blink before he was out the door. Earlier, she'd thought he'd been sending out signals of interest, but then he'd taken off without so much as a goodbye. She couldn't understand it.

Annette had a ready explanation for his abrupt departure. "I bet he had a delayed reaction to getting knocked around and felt queasy. He probably figured that going green about the gills was no way to charm you.''

"What do you mean, charm me?'' Tara had asked.

Annette had giggled. "Come on! There were more sparks flying between you two than at a welders' convention.''

"That's ridiculous,'' Tara had scoffed, but Annette's words had assured her she wasn't imagining that Sam had acted personally interested. But then, why had he rushed off with such a phony-sounding excuse? She was intrigued by the idea of a man with a bit of mystery about him, but wasn't this carrying things too far?

Frowning, she looked out the plane window toward a snowy bank of clouds. One cloud had an outline that resembled a man's profile. It sort of looked like Sam. Annoyed, she turned toward the aisle and saw that breakfast was being served.

She pulled down her tray table and told herself she was going to forget all about Sam Miller. If she'd stayed at home, she would have given him a call, ostensibly about the insurance, but her real motive would have been to try to learn what was going on. But since she wasn't home, she should just forget about him.

Sipping orange juice, she considered the irony of finally taking a vacation just when she'd met an intriguing man back home. With a shudder, she imagined how her brothers would tease if they knew of her predicament. They were a lovable crew, but all too often, their stunts and practical jokes made her want to crawl into a hole. No matter what happened, she could count on them to respond with comic faces, silly puns and wisecracks. Which was exactly why a smooth, aristocratic-looking man like Sam Miller—

Catching herself thinking about Sam again, she finished breakfast, then rested her head back and was able to nap until the captain announced they were to fasten their seat belts for landing.

Well, here I am in Vacation World, Tara thought, entering Miami International, passing groups of suntanned tourists preparing for homeward-bound flights. She saw the baggage claim sign and headed toward it. A girl waving a paper parrot skipped by, her hand held by a woman wearing a T-shirt printed with the words Orchid Jungle. Smiling, Tara anticipated her week. Nothing but sand, palm trees and warm breezes after seeing Opal Carson. With maybe a visit to the home show exhibition at the Coconut Grove Center and some other side trips of interest to decorators. She could almost hear Annette chiding, "Work-work-work." But so what? It was her vacation and she could spend it as she wished.

Tara collected her suitcase from the baggage carousel and wheeled it to the car rental desk. She signed for the car Mrs. Hazelton had ordered and was leaving with the completed paperwork in her hands when she heard a familiar male voice.

"It's about time you showed up someplace where I'm looking."

Gasping, she spun around. There stood Sam Miller, carrying a duffel bag over one shoulder and looking fantastic, dressed in snug-fitting jeans and a striped oxford shirt with rolled sleeves: the cosmopolitan male on casual holiday.

He grinned. "When I couldn't find you anywhere, I started wondering if I'd caught the wrong flight."

"Wrong flight for what?" She was entranced anew by the perfect cut of his dark hair, the sculptured lines of his face, the warm glow in his long-lashed cinnamon-colored eyes.

"Wrong flight to meet you, of course."

"To meet me?" Flustered, she took a step back. Her suitcase started rolling and she had to yank the strap to keep it from bumping into a blue bag that belonged to a heavy-set couple who stood nearby.

"Heel, boy," Sam said with a chuckle.

Clutching the strap, which, thanks to Sam's comment, suddenly *did* seem like a dog's leash, Tara tried to get her thoughts in order. What was he doing here? He hadn't really followed her, had he? She didn't know what to think.

As if reading her mind, he said reassuringly, "I realize how confused you must feel. Let's go someplace quiet and I'll explain." He hesitated, then added softly, "Look, all I'm really after is the Bonbon Ring."

Tara blinked. *Bonbering?* What in the world was "bon-bering"? She'd never heard the word before—it didn't even sound like English.

"You didn't realize anyone else knew about this, did you?" he said, his tone sympathetic. "But I know, so there's no use pretending. You're probably convinced you're doing some friend a favor, but it's a lot more serious than that." He gave a furtive glance around, then leaned closer. "Did you realize that the jewelry was stolen?"

"Stolen?" she echoed. At least that was a word she understood. Not that it made any sense.

"Shh," he cautioned, glancing at the nearby couple, who fortunately were paying no attention. "You had no idea, did you?" He sounded pleased. "That's exactly what I'd decided about you back in the showroom."

All at once, Tara thought she understood. "You're making this up as you go along, aren't you?" She started to laugh. "It's a ploy, an opening line." She'd finally figured out what must be going on, and although its craziness made her a little uncomfortable, it also made her heart flutter. He'd been so attracted to her that he hadn't wanted to wait until she returned home to see her again. Super State Insurance must have a branch office in Miami, and he'd finagled

an excuse to fly down because of her. What a romantic thing
for him to have done.

It was his turn to look baffled. "You know I'm not making anything up. Look, you don't have to be afraid of me.
Like I said, all I'm after is the Bonbon Ring."

She frowned. "You're saying 'ring'? 'Bonbon Ring'?"

"Right." He chuckled. "You didn't even know the name
of it, did you?" He pointed to his thumb. "Big—looks like
it's made for a man, but it's actually for a woman's thumb.
A whopping big ruby on the top, right?"

"Wrong," she said slowly, realizing how serious he
sounded. Maybe his talk wasn't a line after all. "I don't have
the faintest notion what you're talking about."

"But the stuff's stolen!" he whispered in a frustrated hiss.

"What stuff?" He *was* serious. "You're not making—"

"Come on," he argued. "Can't you see I'm trying to help
you?"

She suddenly knew for sure that she'd been all wrong
about him. He believed she had some sort of information
that he wanted. All those warm vibes she'd sensed in the
showroom had been interest in some ring, not in her. Her
face burned. Imagine, thinking he'd followed her to Florida for romance!

"Let's go have coffee and get things straightened out," he
said persuasively. He reached for her suitcase.

Tara had no idea what they could "straighten out" and
she couldn't care less. She felt like a fool and her only de-
sire at the moment was to put distance between them—and
she knew exactly how to do it.

"No, no," she said, moving her bag out of his reach.
"Take this one." She snatched up the tow strap of the blue
bag and placed it into his hand.

He grinned. "Am I leading Rover or Spot?"

Her smile was saccharine. "I call that one Killer."

Turning, she walked off swiftly, pulling along her bag.

"Hey, wait," he called, starting after her. "There's a coffee shop right over—"

"Where do you think you're going?" the woman who owned the blue bag cried indignantly. "Where are you going with my luggage? Horace—this man is stealing our suitcase!"

Sam stammered, "But—but—this isn't— I mean—"

"What exactly *do* you mean?" the woman's husband asked belligerently. He was a broad-chested man with a convention badge on the lapel of his business suit. "Let's hear it. What's your story?"

Sam stared at the angry couple. Their red-faced outrage warned him they wouldn't be easily mollified.

"Well?" demanded the man.

Sam was struggling for a fitting response when another couple, the man also wearing a convention badge, trotted up, their manner radiating good cheer.

"Horace! Millicent! All set for a great two days?" They threw their arms around the first couple in exuberant greeting.

Gratefully escaping in the confusion, Sam mingled with the crowd from a newly landed flight. Emerging on the other side, he looked around in dismay. Tara was nowhere in sight. His stomach clenched. He'd managed to learn from her assistant which flight she would be on, but now he'd lost her. Then he remembered that he'd found her at the car rental counter. Maybe she'd gone for her car. He saw a rental pickup arrow. Sprinting outside, he saw her waiting at the curb as a yellow sedan pulled to a stop before her.

"Hey, Tara," he called. "Wait up." He saw her surprised expression at seeing him again so soon. He grinned to himself as he hurried to her. She would have to learn he could be full of surprises.

"Decided against having that coffee, did you?" he asked, swinging his duffel from his shoulder. "Well, that's okay." He glanced at the yellow car. "Is this what you've rented? I'll explain everything once we're inside and on our way."

Her eyes flashed. "If you think you're going anywhere with me, you've got another think coming." Putting her back to him, she stepped toward the driver, who had just gotten out.

"Nice car," Sam called to the man from over Tara's shoulder.

Tara threw him an angry glance. "Buzz off," she muttered through her teeth, then turned to hand the driver a copy of the rental papers. When the man picked up her suitcase and overnight bag, Sam walked to the trunk with him, making conversation.

"Ever do chauffeur work?"

"There've been a few times," the man answered.

Sam saw Tara watching him with narrowed eyes. He slipped a bill from his pocket. The moment the driver put Tara's luggage into the trunk, Sam said, "I'll get the rest," and handed the man a tip. As he'd figured, the driver assumed that he and Tara were together. He turned over the keys, tipped his cap and left.

Belatedly realizing what had happened, Tara hurried up, but not quickly enough to stop Sam from tossing his duffel into the trunk along with her things and closing the lid.

"All packed," he said with a grin, seeing the angry flush that colored her cheeks. "It's too bad I couldn't get that blue bag you wanted so much, but the lady just wouldn't let go."

He saw the corners of Tara's lips tremble and he knew she was on the verge of laughter, but then her mouth turned grim.

"This has gone far enough," she said. "Either hand over those keys or I call for help."

Sam regretted his impulsiveness. By commandeering her keys, he had been coming on too strong. He'd already scared her with his talk of the gems being stolen. This was no time to upset her further.

"You're right," he told her, and to prove it, he handed over the keys. He saw her eyes widen in surprise. "Believe me," he said, "all I want is a chance to talk with you."

He realized he was taking a calculated risk. Now she could get into the car and drive off and he would be helpless to stop her. On the other hand, regardless of the Whipples' approach, she must have realized there was something shady about shipping out the gems. He was counting on her conscience telling her she should at least hear his story. If she didn't help him, he was in big trouble. His only clue was that her contact in Florida was named Opal.

"Please," he begged. "Let me explain. Besides," he added desperately, "you can't just drive off. You've got my toothbrush and clean underwear locked in your trunk."

This time she did laugh. "Lord, you're impossible! All right, get in the car. You buy me a cup of coffee and I'll listen to your story." Then her eyes narrowed as she looked at the yellow sedan. "By the way, if there are any existing bangs or scrapes and the rental company tries to charge me, you're responsible. You were so smart sending off that driver. I never had a chance to examine the car."

He stared at her, fascinated. "You would have done that? Checked out the car?"

"There's a right way and a wrong way to do things in business," she answered primly. "Besides, it's something my brothers taught me."

He grinned. "It's a deal. Lead on, McDuff."

They stopped at a restaurant that had a Polynesian decor, with a palm leaf ceiling, carved masks on the walls and bamboo furniture. Seated, Sam started explaining the situation. He was prepared for Tara to keep insisting she didn't know what he was talking about and she proved him right, interrupting almost at once.

"But I've never even *heard* of the Whipple gang."

"I never said you did," he answered patiently. "I think you would have refused to go along if you'd known they were crooks. The third member, Gilbert, the brains of the outfit, was probably the one who approached you, using a phony name. I've heard he's pretty slick, has a way with manners and words. He likes to play the gentleman. He must have made smuggling jewelry sound like a harmless adventure."

"And I was supposed to fall for it?" she said, obviously insulted.

Sam blinked. Instead of accepting the excuses he offered, she was arguing with him. Confused, he asked, "What are you saying—that you knew it was stolen? Did you recognize the ring?"

"No! Look, read my lips—I have never even *heard* of the Bonbon Ring."

Sam rubbed a hand through his hair. "Doggone it, Tara, I saw you with that stash of uncut gems, so why keep denying it?"

"What 'stash'? You mean I'm supposed to have more than the ring?"

He cocked an eyebrow. "It isn't as if I didn't see you carrying them, you know."

"But I never—" Stunned realization crossed her face. "You don't mean those stones in the plastic bag, do you?"

"Yes, the stones in the plastic bag."

"But they were *glass*."

He decided not to argue. "Okay, if that's what the Whipples told you, fine. But I'm telling you they were un-cut gems from the Dwight-Astor safe."

"But they *weren't*." She started to laugh. "What you saw was a bag of gem-cut stained glass."

"Whatever. Let's say that the ruby in the ring is glass, too, okay? The point is, you sent it all to somebody here and I need to know where."

"Telling you won't help. I picked up those stones at a stained glass supply house yesterday on my lunch break. And I mailed them to a highly respected stained glass artist who certainly has no interest in crime."

"Okay, okay." Sam was getting annoyed. She sure took the prize for stubbornness. "Just tell me where you mailed that carton."

"But you're on the wrong trail!" She spread her hands. "Sam, if you'd just listen to me—"

"No, you listen to *me*." Tired of hassling, he glared at her. "Just listen without interrupting, and you'll under-stand why it's to your advantage to cooperate."

"All right!" Returning his glare, she folded her arms. "I'm listening."

Leaning forward, he explained about Freddy Dwight-Astor and the ring. He saw her expression becoming more and more thoughtful. Relieved, he knew he was finally get-ting through.

"So you see," he concluded, "Freddy needs to get the Bonbon back to keep out of trouble with his wife, I want to get it back because I want Freddy's entire account in my portfolio, and you'll benefit by getting it back because Freddy will pay a reward."

"All figured out, huh?" She gave him a calculating look. "So—just for the purpose of argument—if what you say is true, what happens to me when the Whipples learn the ring has disappeared? I'll be in trouble, right?''

"Wrong, but it's a sensible question.'' He realized her pride was keeping her from fully admitting the truth, but at least they were holding a rational discussion. "You don't have to worry. As soon as you tell me where I can find the ring, I'll take over. Besides, the Whipples aren't dangerous. The closest they ever came to hurting anyone was when Moss Whipple knocked me down in your shop.''

"Mmm.'' There was an expression on her face that Sam couldn't read. She was so darned beautiful she made him ache. Although she appeared to be the epitome of cool refinement, he sensed a teasing, rollicking side to her personality. What else could explain that spur-of-the-moment trick with the blue suitcase? The possibilities intrigued him. She was a lady made for laughter, and as soon as he finished extricating her from the mess she'd gotten herself into, they would be free to get to know each other.

"Well?'' he said. "Do we have a deal?''

"You want to know where I shipped that package?''

"Yes.'' He waited breathlessly, then saw her come to a decision.

"Okay.'' She started to smile. "Okay.''

Her smile told him she was as relieved as he was to have it settled. As soon as she'd learned her harmless escapade involved real crime, she'd wanted out, only she wasn't quite ready to admit she'd been used. He was curious to know how Gilbert Whipple had persuaded her to get involved. A pang of jealousy shot through him at the thought that Gilbert might have romanced her into the deal.

"Only one thing,'' she said. "I have to go along with you. The person I mailed the package to will be as surprised as I was to hear about stolen jewels. There's no way you could walk in alone and demand to examine the package.''

"Makes sense." He couldn't have thought of a better excuse to stay together himself. "Where do we go?"

"To Opal Carson's artist's studio."

"Sounds interesting." Opal was the name of her contact—now he knew for sure that she was cooperating. "Where is it?"

"Down on the Keys." Grinning, she picked up her purse. "It will be interesting, all right. In fact, I think you're going to love every minute."

Chapter Three

Opal Carson's home-studio was adjacent to a fishing camp on Key Largo. Following directions the artist had given her, Tara parked near the bait shop. She stepped from the car and saw the crushed shell path that led from the parking space to Opal's tin-roofed cottage. Shading her eyes, she looked toward the blue-green, sunlit Atlantic. Gentle wavelets broke against white coral rock, and the fresh-smelling salt breeze blowing through her hair held no reminders of Philadelphia's November chill.

"It's hard to remember how cold it was back home this morning," Sam said. He'd gotten from the car and stood at her elbow. "It's like we've moved to another world."

"Yes, it is," she agreed, feeling a surge of pleasure that he'd seemed to read her mind. Then she considered how he'd failed to do so about something a lot more important. A bag of valuable jewels indeed. And although he hadn't said so exactly, it was clear he suspected Opal of being in on the dastardly scheme, as well. She couldn't suppress a grin. Boy, was he in for a surprise.

Before leaving Miami, she'd phoned Opal to say they were on their way. The connection had been bad and she'd hung up without asking if the package had arrived. She figured it really didn't matter. Opal would have enough stained glass at her studio to make Sam realize his ridiculous mistake.

He moved closer and Tara felt a delicious little tickle as his sleeve brushed her arm.

"I'm glad you're being sensible about this," he said.

Not sure she was being sensible at all, she gave him a surprised look.

He continued, "About you bringing me here without an argument, I mean. For a while there, I was afraid you would keep insisting you didn't know what I was talking about."

"Oh, that." She widened her eyes innocently. "What you've got to understand, Sam, is that I want this straightened out as much as you do."

"Tara. Tara Linton, is that you?" a voice yoo-hooed from the direction of the cottage. A gray-haired woman wearing a ruffled smock waved cheerfully from the porch.

"That must be Opal." Anticipating what lay ahead, Tara took Sam's arm. "Come on—let's get this show on the road."

"Didn't know you were bringing along a fellow," Opal said after Tara had introduced Sam. The woman had a pointed, foxlike face and round glasses that enlarged her lively brown eyes. She grinned at Sam. "Love having visitors, and a good-looking man is a special treat. I only hope you won't be bored while Tara and I talk business."

Not waiting for his reply, she ushered them into a sunny room where a battered counter held glass cutters, a soldering iron, spools of solder and other paraphernalia. One large window was hung with works of stained glass, and the light striking through them transformed the polished wood floor into a richly hued carpet of colored light. Framed photos were on the wall and Tara recognized a much younger Opal shaking hands with President Eisenhower. Impressed, Tara hoped Sam was impressed, too. Another photo showed Opal standing with a group of familiar-looking men.

Sam whistled in surprise. "Hey! They're the astronauts who went to the moon."

Opal blushed. "My work—memorial panels especially—has gotten me some moments in the spotlight." She looked pleased and embarrassed at the same time. Changing the subject, she gestured toward a tall, rectangular carton that sat near the door. "You sure have good timing," she said to Tara. "The plans and supplies you sent just arrived."

Sam turned so quickly to look at the carton that Tara thought he would claim whiplash.

"Have you opened it yet?" he asked.

"No, I figured I might as well wait until Tara got here and we could go over everything together." Eyes sparkling from behind her glasses, Opal rubbed her hands eagerly. "Now that you're here—let's get started."

Figuring she might as well make Sam stew, Tara decided to hold off opening the carton for a few more minutes. "I have some notes from Mrs. Hazelton here in my tote that we should review first," she said, enjoying Sam's look of frustration.

"Let's work at the counter." Opal cleared a space, shifting aside glass, lead strips and a partly completed picture that showed a fire-breathing dragon wearing an elaborate crown. "Sword and sorcery stuff," she said with a chuckle as she placed the picture on the other side of a grinding stone. "Got to move with the times if you want to stay in business."

Pulling up a bar stool for herself, she indicated that Tara and Sam should do the same, then gave him a quizzical look. "Not that I want to chase you away, young man, but there's always something interesting going on over at the dock. Maybe you'd rather have a look around while we do this?"

"No, no." Sam shook his head. "This is plenty interesting."

His voice held a strange note. Tara tried not to smile. She figured he thought Opal was trying to get rid of him, but he managed to keep a straight face.

Opal shrugged. "Suit yourself." She joined Tara at the counter.

Tara had pulled out her notebook and a packet of photos showing the Hazelton home. As she discussed her client's taste, she became increasingly aware of Sam's puzzling manner. Instead of fidgeting restlessly, which was what she had expected, he'd become increasingly quiet. She couldn't imagine what he was thinking. She decided that making him wait wasn't turning out to be so much fun after all.

She set the photos aside. "Let's open the carton. It has scale drawings of the windows where the panels are to be installed."

"Okay." Opal grinned. "I love getting started on a new project. Keeps me young." She started rummaging through items at the end of the counter. "I've got a knife here somewhere to open the box."

"I'll do it," Sam said, standing and pulling a penknife from his pocket. He shot Tara a look she couldn't read, then went to the carton. He placed it on the floor and started cutting the tape.

By the time Tara and Opal reached him, he had the lid free, but instead of opening it himself, he stepped back. He gave Tara another one of his unreadable looks and said quietly, "I guess you know what you want."

Tara found herself hesitating. She'd been sure that as soon as the package was open, he would eagerly tear the top off and reach in to grab what he believed was a bag of precious jewels.

She suddenly felt sorry for him. Finding the ring was awfully important to him and in a minute he would discover he'd flown all the way to Florida on a wild-goose chase. To make things worse, he'd gotten himself even farther afield by traveling down to the Keys. Not that it wasn't his own fault, but still, the situation no longer struck her as amusing. With a reluctance she hadn't been prepared for, she opened the lid, expecting the bag to be right on top.

It wasn't there. She realized he must have opened the wrong end. She pulled out the rolled drawings and handed them to Opal. Working her hand around the Styrofoam chips used for packing, she removed the sheets of glass that were in colors and textures that Opal hadn't been able to find in Florida. Then she reached into the bottom of the box, feeling for the bag of colored glass.

All she felt were the Styrofoam chips.

Alarm rippling through her, she scrabbled her hand around, touching all four corners. Nothing. Unable to believe what was happening, she upended the carton. Pieces of Styrofoam tumbled merrily out, but nothing else.

"But it was here!" The bag had to be in the box. Unmindful of the mess she was making worse with each move, she dropped to her knees and searched through the bouncy foam pieces, hoping against hope that the bag of stones was somehow mixed in with them even though she knew it wasn't possible.

Opal, busy stacking the glass sheets on a shelf next to piles of copper foil, asked, "What are you after?"

"The bag of gem-cut glass." Tara was aware that Sam hadn't said a word. Face flaming, she didn't dare look in his direction. "I know they were here," she said desperately. "I put them in myself. I remember doing it, I remember it exactly."

"Don't fuss about it," soothed Opal, who had started to unroll the sketches. "I can always get them from mail order. It's just that since you were sending me other supplies, I figured you might as well include some gem-cuts."

"But you don't understand." Tara was all too aware that Sam hadn't broken his ominous silence. "I know the bag was inside." She gave the box a desperate shake. "I just know—"

"Tara," Sam finally cut in. "It's okay."

At the sound of his voice, she looked up. "They were just glass," she told him, her tone pleading. He wouldn't believe her—why *should* he believe her? He would remain convinced she'd had a bag of stolen jewels—only now, he would simply assume she'd hidden them someplace else.

"It's okay," he repeated, bending forward, touching her arm. He almost seemed to be cautioning her to say no more. "Opal said she can get them from mail order."

"Sure, it will be no problem," Opal agreed, moving to her work counter, her attention on the drawings. "There's no point in getting upset."

"Tara's a perfectionist," Sam said, covering for her. "To a perfectionist, everything is important. Come on—let's pick up this mess." Kneeling, he started sweeping the Styrofoam bits together with his hands and dumping them back into the box.

Thoughts spinning, Tara helped him clean up, then watched as he returned the carton to the corner. Why was he downplaying the missing stones? He should be furious. His calm manner seemed as out of place as a beanbag chair in a French Provincial room. What was he up to?

Opal, too absorbed in the drawings to pay much attention to anything else, asked a question. Tara answered with only half a mind. Her thoughts remained on Sam, who'd turned to the window, his profile in sharp relief against the light. She could see tension in the set of his shoulders, but his face revealed none of the anger she expected under the circumstances. What was he thinking?

A few minutes later, as Opal showed them to the door, she asked Tara where she would be staying in Miami.

"At a hotel called the Fiesta."

"Okay," Opal said, waving a hand, shooing them out to the porch. "I'll be in touch if I need more information." It was clear she couldn't wait to be alone and start working. "Glad to meet the two of you—have a great vacation, you hear?" The door closed behind them.

Back rigid, Tara stepped off the porch. The sun was still high in the sky, but that light that had felt so bright and warm on her skin now felt chill. Walking along beside Sam on the shell path, she was trying to think of something to say when he interrupted her thoughts.

"You really must think I'm a fool."

Tara set her chin. "It wasn't a trick, no matter how it might have appeared to you." Under the circumstances, she couldn't come up with an adequate defense for herself, but she certainly couldn't allow him to slander Opal. "I have no idea what happened to that bag of stones, but if you think a highly respected artist like Opal Carson sneaked them out and resealed that box, then—"

"Wait a minute." He pulled up short and stared at her. "I don't think anything like that."

"Then what did you mean?"

"That *I*'d been a fool." Seeing her expression, he started to laugh. "Opal turned out to be exactly what you said she was, and as soon as I saw the glass gems in that dragon panel, I knew for sure you'd been telling the truth. Cut glass stones actually do resemble jewels—at least from a distance."

"Then you believe me?"

"Yes, and I owe you an apology. I wanted to find the Bonbon Ring so badly that I talked myself into thinking I was following a great lead even though my gut instincts had been against it all along."

"What gut instincts?"

"About you." His eyes became warm. "Even though I wanted to believe it badly enough to convince myself, I couldn't see you having anything to do with Elmo and Moss. No matter how slick Gilbert's line was, those two would have put too many questions in your mind."

The look he was giving her made her pulse flutter. Moistening her lips with her tongue, she said, "But when I opened that carton and the bag wasn't there, I was so sure you'd think—"

"No, no." He shook his head. "The way Moss and Elmo were running around, the carton probably got knocked over and the bag of stones fell out. I bet if you call home, your assistant will tell you she found it someplace on the floor."

"I suppose that's possible." Tara realized she'd been too upset to speculate how the stones might have gotten out of the box.

Sam tucked his arm in hers as they started walking again, his gesture so easy and natural that she didn't think about it until it had already happened. She sighed inwardly. He was someone she wanted to get to know better, but the natural consequence of their afternoon was that he would want to rush back on the trail of the Whipples. She looked

around, thinking how pretty the scene was. The sea looked
even bluer than before, the salt air smelled even better and
the fronds of a palm tree made soft, whispery noises in the
breeze. A fisherman, dozing in the sun, a hat over his face,
added a picturesque note. Once, she'd thought that a vacation alone was going to be wonderful, but now, all she could
think of was how lonely she would be after Sam left.

As they drove north along the Overland Highway, Sam
fell silent again, and by the time they left the Keys behind,
the quiet had gotten on Tara's nerves. Her attempts at conversation were returned with monosyllables, and the only
music she could find on the car radio was heavy metal or
country and western, neither of which suited her mood. A
glance at Sam showed his handsome face wore a gloomy
expression. She was positive that any minute, he was going
to ask her to drive him back to the airport. Why didn't he
just get it over with? Unable to stand his brooding silence,
she was about to make the offer on her own when he asked
abruptly, ''Where's the Fiesta hotel?''

''It's on the beach in Miami.'' Relieved that they were
talking again, she rattled on. ''Mrs. Hazelton said it was one
of the newer resort hotels—not super elegant, like some of
the famous old places, but more casual and fun.'' She knew
she was babbling and realized she was trying to put off the
inevitable moment when the subject of the airport came up.
''It's supposed to have a beautiful pool, great food, a sauna
and gym . . . everything to make a vacation really special.''

Sam, tired and discouraged, was thinking how nice the
description sounded. A drink by the pool, a good dinner—
what could be better? The fact that he could be sharing it
with Tara was the icing on the cake. The hell with the
Whipples. Maybe he would feel differently in the morning,
but at the moment, he was resigned to the fact that he would
probably never find the Bonbon.

He looked over at Tara, seeing how the little bit of sun she'd gotten that day had colored her cheeks and brightened her eyes, making her lovelier than ever. He remembered that when they'd walked along the path at the fishing camp, the breeze from the ocean had molded her skirt against her thighs. He imagined her body under her clothing.

Abruptly, he said, "You know what I'd like?"

"I can guess." He heard her give a funny little laugh. "You'd like to get back to Philadelphia as soon as possible."

"Well, no," he said, surprised because it was so far from what he'd been thinking. "What I'd like is to forget about the Bonbon—at least for the evening. You've sold me on the Fiesta."

"I have?" She sounded nonplused and he didn't know if his impulsive decision had pleased her or not. "I figured you'd be wanting to go straight back to the airport."

He shook his head. "Right now, I'm in no mood to even think about the Whipples. What I need is a night off, and as I said, you made the Fiesta sound great."

She gave him a suddenly flirtatious smile. "I was only repeating what Mrs. Hazelton told me. Maybe it's the worst hotel in town—algae in the pool, steam table food."

Sam grinned. Her smile showed him she was glad he was staying. "If the place is awful, we'll at least be risking it together. I don't know what we can do about an algae-green pool, but we can take notebooks to dinner and masquerade as food reviewers. That way, the waiters will at least hustle our food from the steam table while it's still hot. How's that sound?"

"It sounds perfect." The look she gave him sent his imagination on a word search to describe the way she made

him feel—wonderful, fantastic, stupendous . . . able to leap
tall buildings in a single bound.

He was still feeling terrific by the time they reached the
hotel. The building had a Spanish look, with an entrance
through a portico that was filled with hanging flower bas-
kets and tubs of scarlet geraniums. He could see on through
to a rose garden and then to a veranda. Beyond the veranda
was a distant glimpse of the beach and the blue ocean.

"Looks nice," he said. Seeing that the porters were busy
unloading an airport limousine, he suggested, "Why not
drive on to the parking area instead of waiting? I can help
you with your luggage."

Her eyes twinkled. "Yes, you're good with luggage, aren't
you?"

He laughed. "It's one of my specialties—as long as the
bags aren't blue."

"I never did ask how you got away from that couple so
fast," she said after the car was parked. "That lady sounded
pretty annoyed."

"Boy, was she! And her husband was even worse." Explaining how he'd been saved by the timely arrival of people the first couple knew, he took the car keys and opened
the trunk. Dropping the keys in his pocket, he hauled out
their bags.

Tara slipped the strap of her overnight bag over her
shoulder as he took his duffel bag in one hand, her suitcase
in the other. To anyone watching, it would appear they were
spending the vacation together. She found it an appealing
illusion, one she wanted to preserve, even if only for the
evening.

When she checked in at the desk, she learned that her
reservations were for what the hotel referred to as a "cottage." "It's one of our special suites on the ground floor,"

the clerk explained, ringing for a porter. "You'll have to see them for yourself to understand how nice they are."

"Could I get a cottage, too?" Sam asked.

The clerk shook his head. "I'm sorry. There are none available for this evening, but we have some very nice regular rooms."

As the porter collected Tara's bags, Sam looked at the key he'd been given. "Room 111. At least it looks as if we're on the same floor."

"At least we're in the same *hotel*," she pointed out. "They could have been full."

"True enough." He took her arm as they followed the porter down the hall. "I think I'll tag along and see where you'll be before I find my own room. Maybe it's the cottages that are so awful—no closet space, bumpy pillows and sheets that won't stay tucked in."

"We'll see." She'd been eager to see what made the cottages special, but Sam's mention of sheets and pillows sent her imagination off in other, more intriguing directions.

They turned a corner and found themselves on the veranda that had been visible from the street entrance. It opened to a tropical garden with a fountain in its center. They stepped down, seeing what appeared to be individual cottages, with red tile roofs, looking out on the fountain and the sea beyond. The units were actually attached to the main hotel, but a clever planting of palms, hibiscus and vines kept the eye low, creating the effect of a miniature Spanish village clustered about a private garden.

Tara gasped with pleasure. "This is lovely."

The porter smiled. "Our cottage guests are always pleased. Over to the far side is the pool and a bar for cocktails." He shifted his attention to Sam. "Your room is down that hallway. If you would like to wait—"

"Thanks," Sam answered, "but I'll find it. Tara, how about if we meet for cocktails in about an hour?"

She agreed and they parted.

An hour later, dressed in a pink sundress, Tara approached a table set on the lawn near the pool. Several lounge chairs were occupied, but no one was swimming. Taking a chair that faced the beach, she looked out toward distant figures wading in the sea. It was a quiet time of day and the only sound she could hear was guitar music coming faintly from inside the bar and the rustling leaves of the banana palm that shaded her table.

She put down her purse—a white clutch just big enough for a comb, lipstick and a few dollars—and opened the little loose-leaf notebook she used to jot down decorating ideas. There was an unusual jardiniere by the pool and she knew of a client who might like something similar. She sketched the ornamental stand, then frowned. Was she out of her mind? Here she was at a seaside resort with a handsome man about to join her, and all she could do was sit here thinking of clients. Not ten minutes ago, when she'd phoned the shop, Annette had said a prospective new customer had called late the previous day, so eager for her decorating advice she'd given him the Miami number. Tara's first hope had been that the call would come through—it might eventually lead to something good—but now she realized she was being ridiculous. *You're on vacation, dammit,* she rebuked herself, leaning back in her chair.

"Penny for your thoughts," offered Sam, coming up from behind her and sliding a hand along her shoulder.

"I was thinking I shouldn't be thinking of work," she answered, keenly aware of a sensation of warmth where his hand had stroked. "But I did learn that those gem-cuts were still at the shop, just as you'd thought." She'd also learned it had been Annette who had told him which flight she would be on. Annette the matchmaker. As he went around the table, she gave him a long look from behind her sunglasses. His hair was damp and slightly waved from his shower, and his dark blue shirt and snug white cotton trousers fitted him exactly right. It could be that Annette had some good ideas after all.

Taking a seat, he saw the open page of her notebook. "So, I was right when I guessed you were a workaholic."

She wrinkled her nose. "Is that why you told Opal I was a perfectionist? It's really not the same, you know."

"I know. I only wanted to offer an explanation for why you were tearing at that box, but maybe a true perfectionist wouldn't have dumped all the Styrofoam. You sure were upset. I figured there was no sense having Opal think something was wrong—especially when there really wasn't."

A waiter appeared to take their order, and Sam told him, "Bring us the wildest tropical drink you've got."

"What did you do that for?" Tara asked after the waiter left. "You don't know what we're going to get."

"Vacation, Tara. Remember? It's time to cut loose."

She rolled her eyes. "That sounds like the advice I get from Annette. Enjoy, she tells me. Enjoy."

"And is she right? And do you do it?"

Tara looked ruefully down at the sketch page. "I suppose she's right, and I suppose I don't do it. But the situation is different for her. For Annette, the shop is only a job. For me, it's a career."

"But now it's your vacation." Reaching over, Sam closed the notebook and slid it to his side of the table. His eyes twinkled. "I'm not thinking about the Whipples and you're not thinking about decorating ideas. Deal?"

When he smiled as he was doing now, she felt willing to agree with almost anything. "Okay. Deal."

The waiter appeared with two drinks, one in a coconut shell, the other in a pineapple. The straws skewered slices of tropical fruit.

"What do you call these drinks?" Tara asked.

"Fiesta Specials." The waiter placed the pineapple drink before her. "Impressive, no?" His accent was faintly Cuban.

"Impressive, yes," Tara said with a laugh. "Thank you."

"Wild enough?" Sam asked after they'd each taken sips of their drinks.

"Not bad. Mine's a rum fruit punch. Is yours the same, or does it have coconut milk?"

He looked thoughtful. "A little, but maybe it's mostly from just being in the shell." He pushed it toward her. "Here, have a taste."

Curious, she took a sip. "It's about the same. Maybe a trifle sweeter."

"Mmm," he said. "Sweet."

She saw the way he was smiling at her, and she suddenly realized the intimacy of sipping from the straw where his lips had just been. Tilting her head, she was about to speak when she saw his startled expression.

"Give me these a minute," he said, reaching toward her. Before she realized what was happening, he'd pulled off her sunglasses and slipped them on his own face. Then he ruffled his hair, making it bushy.

"What in the world—" She stared at him, her mouth open. Her sunglasses were a bright pink with tilted, Fifties-style lenses that looked absolutely ridiculous on a man's face. And his hair! With a gesture that had taken him less than a second, he'd turned a perfect haircut into a joke.

Not bothering to analyze why his actions annoyed her so much, she reached for her glasses. "Take those off—they look stupid." Her tone had a sharp edge. "Completely stupid."

"No, no!" He fended off her hand. Casting a frantic glance behind her, he whispered, "Those people coming this way... Don't look!" He spoke through his teeth. "They're the ones from the airport—the ones with the blue suitcase."

She suddenly understood. Hearing voices, she angled about so she could see. A heavyset couple were greeting a woman who sat in a lounge chair.

Tara turned back to Sam. God, he looked preposterous, but at least it was for a good reason. "They can't be staying here," she said. "That would be too awful." Awful indeed. Next, Sam would be asking for her eyebrow pencil to scribble on a mustache. "They're probably just visiting someone."

"Let's hope so." He stood, keeping his back to the pool. "Come on." He took her arm. "Let's get inside the bar."

"My drink—"

"We'll get more. Come on."

Inside the bar, they looked back through the tinted window, seeing the couple still talking with the woman by the pool.

"I don't think they even glanced our way," Tara said, turning to Sam.

He chuckled. "I guess I risked calling more attention to myself by running than if I'd just stayed put."

Remembering how they'd acted, they simultaneously burst into laughter and couldn't seem to stop.

"Like a pair of fugitives," Tara said, her sides aching.

"Bonnie and Clyde, on the lam." Sam took off the pink glasses. He'd laughed so hard that tears had come into his eyes. "Boy, did I panic. I don't know what I thought they were going to do." Handing the glasses to Tara, he wiped his eyes. "They only saw me for a few seconds in the airport—they probably wouldn't have recognized me, disguise or not."

"I'm sure you're right." She gave him a look, then opened her purse. Putting her sunglasses inside, she said, "You can probably fix your hair now."

"Oh, can I?"

She glanced up, seeing he was already combing it with his fingers. It took only that, plus a good shake of his head and another quick smoothing to put every hair back in place.

"Better?" He was grinning.

"Yes, fine." His grin made her feel foolish. What had she been thinking—that he was going to keep on wearing his hair like a rat's nest? She looked out the window. "They're still out there."

"That's our signal for another drink."

When seated, Sam told her about a nearby tourist site called Coral Castle, built single-handedly out of coral rock by a man still desperately in love with the woman who'd jilted him. It sounded poignantly sad and romantic and Sam said that if she wasn't going to go to stock car races at Hialeah or the Biscayne dog track or *something*, she should at least see Coral Castle. She agreed she might. She wasn't going to mention possible plans to see places of interest to decorators and hear him repeat the word "workaholic."

A good twenty minutes went by before she thought to look out the window again. They'd been having such a pleasant time laughing and talking that she'd forgotten about the blue suitcase people.

"They're gone," she said, turning back to the table. "Not that it matters. As you said, they probably wouldn't recognize you anyway."

During their conversation, Sam had taken a brandy snifter filled with book matches from the bar and had idly started playing with them. She hadn't paid much attention, but now, as she turned back to him, she saw he'd set matchbooks on end to make a platform. He was building a tower. *God,* she thought, cringing, *why do men do things like that?*

"Clever," she said, hoping her compliment would make him stop where he was. "That's quite a talent you've got there."

"I'm a guy with a multitude of talents. My best high school subjects were gym, girls and matchbook building—" he winked "—not necessarily in that order." He started on another tier.

Tara bit her lip, liking the situation less and less. Nearby tables were filling up, but a quick look around assured her that no one was paying attention to the tower—yet.

"That's tall enough, isn't it?"

He studied it speculatively. "Yes, I think so."

She was relieved until he lifted his glass of water.

"Oh, no!"

"Trust me."

"*No.* I—" She knew if she checked now, people would be staring. Shenanigans like this always attracted attention—and always ended in disaster. Her stomach tightened in a knot. He'd built a tower like some damned Babylonian monstrosity and the whole thing was going to end up in a flood. She just knew it.

Tensely, she watched as he moved the glass toward the tower. It was three-quarters full and the ice cubes inside rocked gently. She could predict the next few seconds as if peering in a crystal ball—Sam would position the glass, the tower would collapse and water would spill all over the place.

"No," she said, "I can't just—" She couldn't sit there
and watch, couldn't be part of such dumb antics. Moving
with sudden decision, she pushed back her chair and got up.

The same instant in which she stood, Sam took his hands
from the glass. "Voilà!" he said with a dramatic flourish.
Everything held steady—or at least would have if Tara
hadn't bumped the table.

Sam jumped to snatch the water glass in midair as the
tower collapsed underneath it. He was quick, but not quick
enough to keep most of the water from spilling.

Tara heard gasps from the people sitting nearby. She
stared in dismay at the tableful of soaked matchbooks. Face
flaming, she couldn't meet Sam's eyes. His stunt had ended
up a mess all right, but regardless of who had started it, she
was the one responsible for the grand finale.

Mortified, she turned and fled the bar.

Sam stared after her retreating figure. *Oh, God,* he
thought, *I blew it.* He'd sensed that the tower was making
her uneasy, so why had he kept building it higher? Grand-
standing with the water glass had been the final straw. She'd
been embarrassed. That's what had happened, he'd embarrassed her. *Well, la-di-da.* He started to feel angry. It
wouldn't do to shake up the classy lady and make her feel
foolish, now would it? Finding he still held the nearly empty
glass, he toasted the now empty doorway. *Here's to you, my
prim Miss Tara Linton.* He set down the glass, his mood
shifting back to regret. Tara was the most enticing woman
he'd ever met, and now he'd blown it. They'd made plans
to have dinner together, but at this point, dinner was probably off.

But, dammit, he hadn't done anything wrong. Making
soda straw bridges and matchbook towers was a pastime
with him. She should see the nifty playing card castles he

built one-handed while waiting on hold on the office phone. She shouldn't be so cussed uptight. Especially on vacation.

He remembered her notebook, which he'd stuffed into the waistband of his trousers when they'd run inside the bar. Scowling, he found the page where she'd sketched a flower jug. Her work assignment had been finished after she'd met with the artist, but could she remember she was on vacation? Hell, no, she had to keep right on slaving away.

He leafed through the pages. Blank stationery, a book of stamps, plus an envelope marked "Stamps" and several business cards were tucked in the address section. He saw she'd filled in the addresses with a neat, regimented hand, but when he flipped back to the sketch, he noticed how loose and creative the lines were. Cheered, he closed the notebook. She had it in her to enjoy life, all right—the trouble was, she didn't give herself permission to do it.

He grinned. Enjoying herself was something she should learn, and he was just the man to teach it to her.

Chapter Four

Tara headed toward the sea. There were only a few people on the beach—an older man and woman wearing beach coats, their arms around each other's waists as they stood looking out over the water, and two children playing in the sand close by their mother, who lay reading a magazine. Walking away from them, Tara found a place on the far side of a palm tree, hidden from view of the hotel in case Sam tried to follow.

Sitting, she clasped her arms around her updrawn knees and looked out over the water. Far out, she saw a leaping shape that she thought must be a dolphin at play. The older couple probably saw it, too, as the woman pointed. Tara sighed. The sky was as blue and the water as blue green as the best travel brochure picture she'd been poring over for the past few days, but she found no pleasure in the scene.

She couldn't believe how she'd run away. It had been utterly juvenile. But no more juvenile than Sam had acted. That dumb, show-off tower. For his next feat, he'd probably planned to light a match to it. Under his handsome, polished exterior, he was exactly like her brothers. What a depressing trick of fate.

Sighing, she remembered he had mentioned he'd gotten reservations to fly back to Philadelphia in the morning. With him in Miami for only the night, she supposed she might as well follow Annette's philosophy and enjoy the evening for whatever it was worth. That is, if he still wanted to be with her after the way she'd run off, she thought with a frown.

Getting up, she brushed sand from her skirt and walked back toward the bar, keeping an eye out for him. He was nowhere around, and except for those having predinner cocktails, the beach side of the hotel seemed deserted. It seemed likely that he'd gone to his room. She returned to her cottage, deciding that her best bet was to call him and see which way the wind blew.

She was about to use the phone in her sitting room when a glance into the bedroom made her pause. Her overnight bag sat on the luggage rack, but hadn't she left it on the chair? Frowning, she moved to the bedroom door. Everything was as she remembered leaving it, except for the bag. Feeling increasingly uneasy, she went in and opened the drawer where she'd put her valuables. Her heart started to pound. Her things were all there, only she knew she hadn't shoved them so far back inside. Catching the scent of her talcum power, she looked toward the bathroom. Fear rippled down her spine. The door was now half-closed, but she'd left it open. Whoever had been in her room might still be there, hiding in the bathroom.

For a long, paralyzed second she remained frozen, then her body came to life. Wheeling about, she raced outside, not taking the time to close the cottage door. She stumbled through the deserted garden and up the veranda steps, then looked back. There was nobody after her, nobody running away. She didn't know what to do. A house phone caught her eye. She grabbed the receiver and asked the operator to connect her with Sam's room.

"Somebody broke into my cottage!" she blurted as soon as he answered.

"What? What do you mean?"

"Somebody was there. He might even still be inside."

"Tara . . . where are you now?"

"On the veranda. There's a house phone—"

"Wait right there!"

While waiting, she paced, keeping an uneasy eye on her cottage. Her throat felt dry and she shivered despite the warmth of the evening air. The lights hidden in the thick leaves of exotic foliage around the fountain had been switched on. Normally, she would have found the play of light and shadow romantic, but in her present mood, it only struck her as eerie.

Footsteps hurried along the tiled hallway and Sam appeared.

"Thank God," she said, rushing to him.

"Are you all right?" He took her into his arms. "You're trembling."

She relaxed against him. It felt wonderful to be held. Against his shoulder, she said, "I'm all right. It was just so awful to know that someone had . . . had *invaded* my room. And then I got to thinking he still might be there."

"I'll check it out." Sam's voice took on a tough note. "Which cottage is yours—the open door?"

"Yes, but don't go alone." She clutched his arm. "It may be dangerous."

"I'll be all right. Just wait here."

He strode off. Torn between running for help and running after him, Tara stayed where she was. Sam disappeared inside the cottage. A moment later, he emerged. "Everything is fine," he called.

"You checked everywhere?"

She didn't hear his reply because of a rustling in the bushes. A small figure suddenly darted out from behind a hedge near the fountain. Startled, Tara realized she was seeing a boy about twelve years old. He scrambled up the steps and hurtled toward her.

"Look out!" she cried, trying to dodge out of his way.

"Look out yourself, lady," the boy retorted, snatching her purse.

"Hey!" Sam called, seeing what happened. He ran toward the veranda. "Stop! Drop that purse!"

Together, Sam and Tara ran after the boy. Always able to give her brothers a good run for their money, Tara kept pace with Sam as they reached the street. The boy had disappeared.

Out of breath, she cried, "Did we lose him?"

"Afraid so." Hands on his lean hips, Sam stood peering up and down the street.

Tara suddenly caught sight of the small figure. "There he is, in the parking lot!"

"We'll get him this time." Sam took off again. They were almost to the lot when Tara suddenly caught sight of a white car careening from the side of the area and heading straight toward them.

"Watch it!" She grabbed the back of Sam's shirt, yanking him out of harm's way.

Sam's mouth fell open as the car zoomed past. "That driver! We've got to go after him."

"We'll take my car," she began, then grimaced. "Oh, no—my car keys must be in my purse."

"No, they're not." Sam pulled them from his pocket. "I still have them. Come on, we can't let them get away."

"What about the driver of that car?" She flung herself into the passenger seat and yanked her skirt free from the closing door. "You sounded so shocked—was the boy driving?"

"No." Sam slammed his own door. "The driver looked like Moss Whipple."

"What?" Tara stared at him. "Why would that crook show up here?"

"That's what I want to find out." He twisted to look out the back window. "All-right-a-rooney! Fasten your seat belt, 'cause here we go." He whirled the car out of its slot.

All-right-a-rooney? Tara thought as they tore out onto the main street. Next, he would be saying, "Shazam."

There wasn't much traffic and the white car showed up easily in the twilight. Speeding, they crossed a number of streets, managing to keep the light-colored car in view.

"You know it can't be Moss," she reasoned when she could talk again after they'd zoomed around a tight corner nearly on two wheels. "It makes no sense to have him here."

"I know that, but it sure looked like him." The white car made a turn. Sam turned, too, going against a red light, inadvertently cutting off a Jeep that had just gotten the signal to go. Cringing, Tara heard an angry horn sounding behind them as they barreled into a narrow side street. She had no sooner gotten the nerve to look up again when she saw the white car screeching to a stop directly ahead.

"Look out!" she yelled.

Avoiding a crash, Sam swerved, fighting to keep control as they rocketed past.

Heart in her throat, Tara twisted to look out the back window.

"Are they backing up?" Sam yelled, stomping the brakes, coming to a stop.

Tara found her voice. "They're just sitting there. No...the boy's jumping out. He's running this way. He's bringing my purse!"

Sure enough, the youth, waving her purse in the air, was running toward them. Just as Sam started to get out, the boy darted past their car, tossed the purse to the street in front of their bumper and kept on running.

"My purse!" Without thinking, Tara burst from the car. By the time she'd recovered the purse—it was empty, of course—she heard an engine roar. She looked up to see the white car backing from the narrow street. Tires screeching, the driver reversed gears and tore off.

"It was a ruse," she spat in disgust as she slid back into her seat. "The stuff in my purse is gone, the boy's gone, the car's gone...." She slammed the door. "A sleazy trick, and I fell for it."

"We both fell for it," Sam corrected her. "I got out of the car, too." Frustrated, he looked back down the narrow street. "Damn, but that driver looked like Moss."

"You know that's impossible."

"Yeah, you're right. What a mess. What did they get from your purse?"

"Not much, just a few dollars and some cosmetics. This is just a little sport purse. My wallet and other stuff are safe in my room. I saw them when I checked my jewelry."

"Hey, great—that's a break." He started the car moving again. "You know what I think? I bet that kid, the purse snatcher, was the same one who got into your room. He's probably part of a gang where an adult uses youngsters to rob tourists."

"Oh, like Fagin in *Oliver Twist*. Only why didn't he take my valuables then? He rummaged through the drawer—he had to have seen them."

"Maybe he's new at the game and got rattled. In any case, I bet the hotel desk clerk will tell us there's a gang like that working the area."

But back at the Fiesta, when they reported Tara's rifled room and the purse snatching, the clerk denied all knowledge of such a gang.

"There are, regrettably, isolated incidents, but certainly nothing organized," the man said, his manner apologetic, but firm in the conviction that no gang existed. After taking information for a police report, he readily agreed with Tara's request to have her room changed, only he explained he couldn't switch her to another cottage until the following day. "I'll give you a nice second-floor room for tonight," he said. "And then in the morning, another cottage should be available. Is that satisfactory?"

She nodded. "That's fine, thanks. Just as long as I don't have to stay in a place that's been broken into."

A few moments later, as Sam accompanied Tara to the cottage to help move her things, he grumbled, "I still bet there's a gang working the area. The hotel just refuses to admit it."

"I can't say that I blame them. What matters is that they make sure to beef up the security."

After her things had been transferred to her new room, Tara was starving and she figured Sam must be starving, too. And she certainly owed him something for everything he'd done. "How about being my guest for dinner? Anything from the steam table that your little heart desires."

His eyes twinkled. "Actually, the restaurant is probably a gourmet heaven, but I've made reservations for someplace else. That is," he added mischievously, "if you're still willing to go out with me. I promise to restrain myself—no more balancing water glasses."

"Okay," she said, figuring the concession was about the best she could ask for. "And I shouldn't have bolted like I did. Spilling that water—I was the one who made the mess."

He shrugged and grinned. "All part of the fun."

He *would* see it that way, she thought, giving him a patient smile. "Just let me get changed—I didn't get a chance to do a thing before." She looked at her watch. "I'll meet you in the lobby in fifteen minutes."

It ended up taking her nearly a half an hour, but when she entered the lobby wearing an off-white Indian gauze dress with lace inserts, the look in Sam's eyes assured her that her time had been well spent.

"Lovely," he said in a soft voice, giving her his arm.

"Thanks." They might have a nice evening after all. And as Annette would say, it was only an evening.

The restaurant Sam had selected had an Art Deco flavor, with a red-and-black color scheme, chrome accents and modern art on the walls. Between the main course and dessert, they tried the dance floor, swirling under star lights in a mirrored ceiling. After dessert, they danced again.

"This band is terrific," Tara said, out of breath after a spirited "Bring Back the Fifties" medley. She joined the others in applauding the leader, a round-faced man with a goatee, who'd called out in a spirited way during the dances to keep things jumping. Twice, he and the band's pretty, redheaded vocalist had joined the others on the floor and performed dances of their own.

"So, you're really having fun?" Sam asked.

Tara shot him a grin. "You need to ask?" Laughing, she made a futile attempt at smoothing her hair, which floated about her flushed face.

The next dance was a slow one and they decided to sit it out and have some refreshments. Walking back to their table, Tara compared the formal restraint of the dining area—

where their French cuisine had been served by an impeccable waiter—with the liveliness of the dance floor. The es-
tablishment was as much of a paradox as Sam: an exuberant
all-right-a-rooney guy one moment, a suave gentleman the
next.

At their table he smiled and lifted his glass in a toast.
"Here's to you and vacation. I think you've finally decided
it's okay to really believe you're off on a holiday."

Tara thought he looked proud of himself, as if he was
convinced he'd single-handedly brought about her changed
attitude. To be honest, she supposed he had. Nothing like a
car chase to make a woman forget the dull routine back at
home. She saw the sparkle in his eyes and the smile that
brightened his lean, aristocratic features. God, it was almost a sin for a man to look so appealing. She remembered
he'd handled the tricky driving maneuvers with the skill of
a James Bond. She found the image surprisingly sexy.
Maybe she had more of a yen for adventure than she realized.

"What will you do for the rest of the week?" he asked.

"Nothing much except taking it easy." Her plans to
mostly laze around the resort hotel with a peek or two at
some decorating stuff suddenly seemed awfully bland. She
gave him a curious look. "If this were your vacation, would
you have planned a lot of activities?"

"Maybe. Like what?"

"Oh…" She envisioned the kind of holiday her brothers
would want—anything to keep the action going. "You
mentioned the car races, the tracks…then there's fishing,
sailing, scuba diving, that sort of thing."

He nodded. "Sure. On a vacation alone you have to give
yourself something to do."

She smiled. "My main 'something' is going to be to lie in the sun and read a juicy novel." So much for her yen for adventure.

He lifted an eyebrow. "If all you wanted was to get a tan and read a book, you could have stayed in Philadelphia under a sun lamp. The way you're going about it, you won't see anything of Florida."

She shrugged. "I went down to the Keys, didn't I?"

"Sure, in connection with your work. You didn't really see anything except from your car window."

"I was at that fishing camp, and I saw the ocean," she said defensively. Hearing herself, she realized how ridiculous her argument sounded. Grinning, she amended, "In connection with my work, I walked past a fishing camp and took a look at the ocean."

He laughed. "Gosh, how could I have forgotten your big sight-seeing excursion?" He got to his feet. "Back to the dance floor for us. For at least one night in Miami, you're going to do something besides watch the world go by."

An old song was playing. As Tara moved effortlessly with Sam to the dreamy melody, she was thrillingly aware of the warmth of his body against hers. No question about it, she liked being in his arms.

"I'd wondered how it would be to slow dance with you," he said against her ear.

Tipping her head back, she smiled. "Does the reality live up to your expectations?"

"It's even better. Almost as if we've practiced."

"In another lifetime, perhaps?" she teased.

He chuckled, and she could feel the movement of his chest against her breasts. "You think I'd try that old reincarnation line?" His breath was warm against her lips. "Haven't I met you somewhere, perhaps in another age? You and I, floating down the Nile in ancient Egypt. You and

I, having a forbidden tryst in a perfumed garden in old Baghdad.''

"Mmm, you're making living lots of lives sound romantic.''

"I am, aren't I? But when I said it's like we've practiced, reincarnation wasn't what I had in mind.''

"What *did* you mean?''

"That maybe you'd been imagining what it would be like to dance with me.'' His mouth was so close to hers that if either of them moved a fraction, their lips would meet. "And because we'd both been thinking about it, it was inevitable that it would seem exactly right when it finally happened.''

She answered with provocative softness. "Then you're saying this seems exactly right?''

The circle of his arm tightened, bringing her closer. He looked into her eyes. "Isn't it?''

She didn't reply, but the rapid pace of her pulse and the weakness in her legs made the answer almost painfully clear. Her intellect might have had doubts about him being the man she wanted, but her body didn't have a qualm.

Without warning, the tempo of the music changed. The bandleader called out, "Come on, little fishes, swim! Swim 'The Fish.' '' The music swung into a dance that required vigorous swimming motions.

Confused by the swift change of pace, Sam turned to look toward the band. A disappointed Tara stood with her arms at her sides. This number was too much of a show-off for her, especially when she'd been in such a different mood. Returning to their table seemed like a good idea and she was about to say so when she saw that the bandleader had left his stand again and now mingled with the couples on the floor. He swung a laughing gray-haired woman around while her partner cheered, then he released her to "swim" on through the crowd, his goatee bobbing as he urged the dancers on. His eyes suddenly locked with hers. Tara felt her mouth go dry. Her inactivity had singled her out. Dear Lord, was the man coming to her? She would die if he tried to swing her around in public....

Sam, who'd also noticed the direction of the bandleader's gaze, saw Tara's expression. It looked as if she were wishing the floor would open up.

Sam hesitated for only a second, then grabbed her hands. "Up over the waves, little fish!"

Forcing her stiff arms up and down, he turned her so her back was to the bandleader. "That's it, that's it, get your fins in gear," he encouraged softly, stepping in time to the music as he angled her through the gyrating dancers and away from the bandleader. He felt her start to move more easily.

Saved, she thought with relief. Peering past the other dancers, she saw the bandleader dancing with a lady who clearly relished the attention. She smiled up at Sam, feeling she could breathe again. He'd released her hands and continued the swimming motions in a low-key way. He obviously wasn't hating the dance and she supposed she wouldn't really hate doing it with him. It was being singled out that would have bothered her—to think some people would have loved it! The dance was silly but harmless. She might as well be a good sport.

When she started "swimming," Sam felt bubbles of delight effervesce through him. She must have decided that if she was going to dance crazy, it might as well be with him. She looked so beautiful, he thought, her short blond hair fanning about her face, her lacy white dress billowing. It seemed that she'd finally cast all her cares to the wind.

The dance was nearly over and Tara had to admit that she had enjoyed herself when the bandleader, back on the stand again, waved one of the restaurant's red napkins and cried, "The Bull!" The trumpet sounded the traditional fanfare to a bullfight.

Oh, no, she thought with tolerant dismay as men began hunching their shoulders and positioning their fingers to make horns on their head. She was glad that she and Sam were on the edge of the activity and could easily walk away—especially when someone started passing out red napkins for the women to use as miniature bullfighter's capes.

A napkin was passed to Sam. "Olé?" he questioned, extending the cloth to her.

Laughing, Tara shook her head. Enough was enough. This was where she got off.

Remembering how she'd warmed up to the other number, he decided to take the chance that her laugh was actually a bid for encouragement. "Come on," he encouraged, waving the napkin. "Come on, Tara. I dare you."

He *dared* her? He was really the limit. The situation suddenly struck her as amusing. They were on the rim of the dance floor and everyone was too involved to pay them any attention. If Sam was determined to act like one of her brothers, maybe she ought to return the kind of trick that one of them would appreciate. Not giving herself time to think, she snatched the napkin.

Delighted, Sam mimicked the other men, lowering his head as if preparing to charge. Tara swirled the napkin as he went by her. While his back was still turned, she walked off the floor. He shifted around and looked dumbly at the place where she'd last been. The light dawned. He shifted his gaze and saw her returning to the table.

"I guess that's the last time you'll dare me," she said as he caught up. She smiled as if she was a little surprised with herself but pleased, as well.

"Heck, no," he said with a laugh. "Now that I know you can't refuse a dare, there's no telling what I'll come up with next."

His expression was so deliberately evil that Tara couldn't help laughing. "You're the absolute limit, that's what."

"That veronica was the limit, too." He helped her with her chair, then took his own. "How'd you learn that move?"

She realized he meant the impulsive flourish she'd given the cloth. "I didn't know it was called a veronica. I suppose I saw it in a movie when we were kids."

"We?"

"My three brothers and I. They were always copying rough-and-tumble stuff from movies and TV. Even though I was the youngest, I went right along. We had a rope tied to a maple limb and I'd swing on it and pretend to be a jungle girl."

"Raised by apes, like Tarzan?"

She shrugged. "Sheena of the Jungle, actually. You've got to remember, I was only a kid."

"Sounds wonderful. I was an only child. Having even one brother would have been great. Do you see them often?"

"Fairly often." She tilted her head, smoothing her hair back behind her ear. She was still a little surprised at how she'd acted. And on a dare yet! "Cal's married and the last time we were all together was at his farmhouse at Thanksgiving." Remembering that afternoon, her nose wrinkled as she added, "The predinner event was playing touch football in a muddy cow field."

Sam chuckled. "I take it you didn't join them."

"I stayed in the house with my grandmother."

"Watching the turkey cook."

"No, I decorated the dining table."

"Mmm." His eyes twinkled. "And I bet it looked great. But after you'd finished, wasn't there still time to go outside and cheer the game on?"

"Believe me, that crew hardly needs any encouragement. Cal even had his two-year-old son out there wallowing in the mud."

"And loving every minute."

"I suppose." And Sam would have loved it, too, she thought wryly. Mud and mess and rowdy noise.

Later, when the music turned slow again, they returned to the dance floor. Wrapped in Sam's arms she thought how nice he could be when he tried. She remembered what she'd told him about Thanksgiving. Annette would call her a party pooper. Maybe she was, but so what? It wasn't necessary to hoot and holler in order to have fun. It was the way she honestly felt and Sam finally seemed to have gotten it through his head. They were simply relaxing and having a good time. He swirled her around to the music and moved a caressing hand along her back, pressing her closer. Her thoughts flew as she became increasingly aware of his body against hers. She closed her eyes. She was tired of analyzing things. All she wanted to do was experience the moment, to enjoy the dance.

When they left the restaurant an hour later, Sam, carrying his jacket over one arm, his other arm around Tara's slim waist, reviewed the evening. Her trick with the red napkin had been hilarious. He imagined what his expression must have been like when he turned and found she'd gone back to the table. It made him want to laugh out loud. He didn't think he could ever be bored by such a woman. She'd surprise him at every turn. Not that he didn't have tricks up his own sleeve. Wasn't he getting her to relax, to stop thinking about work? Then he remembered the way she felt in his arms when they'd slow-danced, the way her body had almost seemed to flow against his. Maybe the best thing was that she was relaxing with *him*.

What would it be like if he arranged to stay a few more days in Florida? The trail to the Bonbon Ring was so cold he was only kidding himself to imagine he might find it again. The entire caper had been too much of a long shot anyway. He had work waiting back at the office, but he still had one more day of vacation left. He'd never said for sure that he would be at his desk the next day. . . .

He looked down at Tara as they strolled along the quiet street, heading for the lot where they'd parked their car. Cuddled against his shoulder, she must have felt his gaze, for she glanced up and smiled. His heart seemed to turn over. Had he ever known anyone more lovely? The exertion of dancing had tousled her hair charmingly and her expressive gray eyes held a glow that warmed him clear down to his toes. He wondered how she felt about him. What he longed to do right then and there was to stop right in the middle of the sidewalk and kiss her. How would she respond? He reminded himself to go easy. She had a reserve that warned him against rushing the situation—he didn't want to risk spoiling things.

They turned the corner and Tara said, "I don't remember the parking lot being so dark."

Sam frowned. The lot provided parking for nearby apartments as well as the restaurant, and it should have been well lit. But she was right—the only illumination was from the street lamp on the corner.

"There was one of those big floodlights in the center of the lot," he said. "I can just barely make out the pole. It must have burned out."

"It's a good thing I remember where we left the car," Tara said, shifting to the right.

"Hold on. We're parked to the left."

"To the left?" she questioned.

"That's how I remember it."

She squinted around the dark lot, as if squinting could help. "To the left, huh? And of course, you're right because men always have the best sense of direction."

Laughing, he took her hand. "You're not going to trap me into some feminist argument. First, we'll check the place where *you* think it is."

"I heard that skeptical note in your voice," she teased. They walked slowly. Although the glass and chrome of the parked vehicles reflected the corner lamp, the ground underfoot was in shadow. "You're convinced that I'm wrong and you're right, aren't you?"

"Sure. But only because I *am* right—not because I'm a man."

"Sounds chauvinistic to me," she scolded in a knowing tone. But a few moments later, after exploring the right side of the lot, she had to admit that she'd apparently been mistaken after all. As they turned back, she said, "And it's very nice of you not to say, 'I told you so.'"

"How do you know I won't say it?"

"Because you're a nice person."

"Oh." He grinned in the dimness. "I'm not going to argue that one, either."

As they retraced their steps past the burned-out light, Sam heard something crunching underfoot. He'd noticed the sound before, but this time, he was curious enough to investigate.

Tara, who'd walked on ahead, looked back. "Drop something?"

"No. There's something here...."

As he'd suspected, there was broken glass on the ground. He peered up at the darkened floodlight. It hadn't burned out at all but had been smashed by vandals. A noise caused him to glance in Tara's direction.

"Tara?" He couldn't see her. It was dark, but not so dark that she would simply disappear. Confused, he looked around. He knew where she'd been standing, in front of a couple of parked vans. Maybe she'd decided to cut through the lot by going between them. Only why hadn't she responded to his call?

"Tara?" he called again, moving forward.

He heard a scuffing sound. It came from between the two vans. More scuffling and then what sounded like a muffled cry—

Adrenaline spurted through his system. Not stopping to think, he plunged into the blackness between the vans. A force caught him in the midsection, ramming him backward and knocking him down. He heard Tara scream. His shoulder smacked the cement with a bone-jarring thud. Tara screamed again. He didn't have a chance even to try to get up before his assailant was running over him, tromping across his stomach and chest as if he were some kind of damn freeway. He had a confused realization of something similar happening to him once before. The next thing he knew, Tara was whispering frantically into his ear.

"Sam! Sam...are you all right?" She shook him, making his shoulder hurt like the devil. "Are you all right?"

Coughing, he regained his breath. "Yeah, I think so." Her face was a ghostlike shape in the darkness. He shook his head, clearing his thoughts. "How about you? I heard you scream—"

"When you showed up, it gave me a chance to yell. He ran off, but he might come back." She tugged his arm.

"Damn mugger," Sam mumbled. "Mowed me right down." Tara's tugging was killing his shoulder. "Let me get up myself. No, help me . . . only pull on this arm."

With her assistance, he got to his feet.

"Better let me drive," she said, picking up his dropped jacket.

Not arguing, he handed her the keys, but when they'd reached the car and were safely inside, he noticed she still seemed shaky.

"Are you sure you're all right?" he asked. "I can manage if you're not."

"I'm fine. I just want to get out of here." Her voice was tense. "Nobody's come to investigate the commotion. I won't feel safe until this place is behind us." Once the car was on the street, she took an audible breath. "We should tell the police."

"They can't do anything." It was a spot behind his shoulder, more on his back, that felt weird now. Sam could think only of getting home to his room. "The guy already took off, so what good can the law do? And besides, if we file a full report we could be here for hours."

"It wouldn't hurt to just let the police know. As long as that lot is dark, he may sneak back and wait for somebody else."

Sam admitted she had a point. He saw a police car at the curb up ahead. A uniformed officer stood under a street lamp, writing a ticket for an illegally parked vehicle.

"Pull over by that cop." Sam reached with his good arm to roll down his window. "Officer?" he called as Tara brought the car to a stop. The man looked around and Sam said, "We've just come from a parking lot a couple of blocks back. Vandals have broken the floodlight and we think we saw someone skulking around in the dark. Maybe the place should be checked out."

"Two blocks back, you say?"

"Yes, the parking area behind the restaurant."

"I know the place," the policeman said. "Thanks."

"Do you think that's enough?" Sam asked Tara as he rolled up the window.

"Yes, as long as somebody's alerted." She realized she was still trembling. Getting herself under control, she started the car moving, then glanced over at Sam with concern. "You're hurt, aren't you?"

He rubbed his bruised ribs and gingerly wiggled his shoulder. Yes, the tender spot was definitely more on his back. "It's my pride as much as my bones. That guy ran over me like a steamroller." He cursed softly. "It looks like it's getting to be a fad to knock Sam Miller down and give him a good stomping. Man, what a day! I'm just glad you're all right. When you screamed, I thought you'd been hurt."

"No. He grabbed me and told me to keep quiet, but then you were there, and—"

"He *grabbed* you?"

"Only for a second. I mean, I don't know what might have happened if you hadn't shown up, but you did."

"My God, Tara!"

"Yes, but I'm all right, so...let's not talk about it anymore now, okay?"

Actually, there was something else she was dying to say, but it was so crazy she had to think it over a little more: the mugger had been as chunky as the gum-chewing Moss Whipple. And in addition to that, when he'd clapped a hand over her mouth and said, "Keep quiet, lady, just keep quiet—nobody's supposed to get hurt," she'd clearly smelled spearmint on his breath.

Chapter Five

After what's happened, I'm glad you weren't given another cottage," Sam said as they entered the Fiesta. "The cottages are pretty, but I feel you're a heck of a lot safer in the main part of the hotel."

"I agree." Tara suppressed a shudder as she glanced toward the leaf-shrouded veranda. "Even with you with me, I'd feel uneasy walking along that garden path at night."

"What's that supposed to mean?" he chided with mock hurt feelings. "You think I'm too battered to come to your rescue?"

She remembered how fearlessly he'd come running when she'd needed him. He had his good points; she had to give him that. "No, you're just too battered for me to ask it of you. How do you feel?"

"A good night's sleep should fix me up fine. I'll see you safely upstairs to your room, then—" He broke off, snapping his fingers. "I took your notebook when we were by the pool and I've got it on my desk. We'll stop at my place first and get it."

In his room, Tara saw the back of his shirt and gasped. "You're bleeding!"

He dropped his jacket to a chair and tried to look over his shoulder. "It must be from that three-point landing I made when that bozo ran me down." He tugged at the back of his shirt. "It looks as if the blood has stopped by now."

"If it has, the way you're going at it will start it up again."

"But I can't leave it this way," he said, still tugging.

"Will you stop it! You should put a wet washcloth or something on it first if it's stuck." Lord, he was as bad as her brothers. Men were great at playing macho, but as soon as the excitement was over they turned as helpless as babies.

"Unbutton your shirt," she said, moving to stand behind him. She pulled his shirttail from his trousers and ran her hand up the inside of the fabric, finding she could gently ease it away from the wound. He'd gotten the buttons undone by that time and she was able to peel off his shirt without making further contact with his injury. The palm-sized scrape was low on his shoulder blade and toward the center of his back. Tara winced. "You've got an awfully nasty-looking scrape."

He angled so he could see in the mirror. "Yeah, but it's nothing serious."

"Unless it gets infected. We need something to put on it."

"Maybe I've got something." He lifted his duffel bag and started rummaging through a side compartment, tossing out a deck of playing cards and some travel maps. "I think I stuck in one of those giveaway packets of first aid stuff.... Yeah. Here it is." He opened the packet, revealing a tube of antibiotic ointment, gauze pads and some Band-Aids. "This will do the job."

She nodded. "Yes, only you can't reach around to do the job yourself. Sit on the bed and I'll be back as soon as I've washed my hands."

In the bathroom, Tara was washing her hands when the sight of Sam's shaving kit and toothbrush suddenly made her aware of the intimacy of the situation. She remembered how she'd ordered him around and shucked him out of his shirt. If he hadn't undone the buttons fast enough, she supposed she would have whirled him about and started unfastening them herself. She cringed at the memory. He was enough like her brothers not to pass this one up. Sooner or later, he would make some crack about her eagerness to tear his clothes off. Despite his boisterous streaks, he'd given no signs of crudeness, but this would undoubtedly bring it out.

She decided it was best to treat him exactly like one of the characters she'd grown up with. She efficiently wrung out a warm washcloth and opened the bathroom door. If he wanted to make cracks, so what?

In the bedroom she found he'd switched off the overhead light leaving the room softly illuminated by the desk lamp at the far wall. Seated on the bed, he looked up at her and smiled. The fatigue that had darkened his eyes and made hollows under his cheekbones somehow managed to heighten his natural good looks.

She cast off notions about the dim lighting being romantic and about the bare-chested Sam looking appealing.

"Where's the first aid stuff?" she asked briskly, turning on the bright bedside lamp, telling herself that the only reason he wasn't up to making smart comments was because he was too tired.

"Right here." He indicated the first aid supplies on the night table and shifted his position on the bed so she could easily reach his back. The job of playing nurse was taking on a much more personal aspect now that she was so close and so aware of his smoothly tanned skin and the strong, lean musculature of his shoulders. She stopped the dangerous direction of her thoughts. The wound was deeper than she'd realized, but as she gently sponged it with the cloth, he gave no sign that he felt discomfort.

As she worked, she couldn't help noticing the fine shape of his hairline at the nape of his neck. Not even the most expert barber could take credit for that perfect line, nor his thick hair, with just the slightest suggestion of a wave. The faint scent of his cologne mingled with a pleasant scent that was distinctly his own. With unsteady hands she placed a gauze square over the medicated area and taped the edges.

"There," she said, placing a hand on his good shoulder to let him know she was done.

"Thanks." Reaching up to clasp her hand, he turned to meet her eyes. "You have the gentlest touch," he said softly.

Although he'd made light of it, the scrape on his back had smarted like hell. He'd steeled himself not to wince when she started working on him. Wimping out would have been shameful enough under ordinary conditions, but to a woman with three brothers who sounded like such regular guys it would have been a real turnoff. But when she'd started touching him, the lacy stuff of her dress tickling his bare arms as she leaned forward, his senses had filled with nothing but the awareness of how close she was. He'd held his breath, afraid she would be able to tell how much her nearness was affecting him. It was clear she had nothing on her mind but the care of his injury. He couldn't risk scaring her off by panting like a steam engine.

When she'd finished and rested her hand on his shoulder, he hadn't been able to stop himself from reaching for her. Her hand was cool in his, yet he was sure he'd felt a tremor when he'd enfolded it. Or was the tremor just his own pulse threatening to leap out of control?

"I didn't hurt you, did I?" she asked, sounding anxious. "I tried to be careful."

He shook his head. There was something in her misty eyes that encouraged him, but he couldn't think of anything to say. Instead of speaking, he turned her hand over and kissed her palm. The next thing he knew, she was sitting in his lap. He wasn't sure if he'd pulled her there or if it had just happened. In any case, he was kissing her, which suddenly seemed like the most natural thing in the world to do.

Tara had been too surprised to resist when he'd drawn her into his arms. She found herself cradled on his lap, her palm still tingling from his kiss. He kissed her hand again, then her wrist. Then, his lips, warm and tender, brushed her mouth with a pressure so light it was like a breeze wafting across rose petals.

"You've got the prettiest hair," he murmured, lifting his head, smiling into her eyes. He gently toyed with the silken tendrils that lay along her cheek. "Angel hair. It's like somebody captured the sunlight and spun it into a halo."

She'd been prepared for familiar references to her hair color: corn silk or honey or taffy. His unfamiliar compliment struck her as pure poetry.

She sighed, lifting her arms to circle his neck. She drew him closer, offering her lips to him once again. Time and place and reality retreated. There was only the wonder of Sam's arms and a kiss that went on and on.

Kissing Tara, he thought dreamily. Was there a song called "Kissing Tara"? If not there darned well ought to be. He would write the words and the music, as well, and play it only for her. From the first moment he'd seen her, he'd imagined holding her like this. Dancing with her had been terrific, but this was even better. Far better. He shifted to a half-reclining position and she made no protest as he pulled her down to lie beside him. Making magic with Tara. Her mouth was like moist silk and her soft, slim-waisted body against his was a dream come true.

It wasn't until he reached over and switched off the bedside lamp that Tara became aware of the frantic thudding of her heart and her labored breathing. The excitement and danger of the evening had created a romantic intensity that would never hold up in the light of day. It was time to back off. She struggled to free herself from the spell he'd cast over her.

"Sam . . . Sam, there's something I forgot to tell you."

He cursed silently. Turning off the light had been a bad move. He'd felt her tense and had immediately realized his error. Why had he thought he had clear sailing? He should have known better. Good things didn't come so easily. He calmed down, realizing he was acting like a thwarted kid. Tara was special, a woman he wanted to get to know. He would have to let her set the pace.

"Forgot to tell me what?" he asked with a lazy chuckle. "You're married? Engaged?"

"No." She evaded his kiss. "It's that—"

"You're worried about the insanity in your family, right?" He nuzzled the delicate seashell of her ear. "It's okay. It must be in mine, too, because I'm crazy about you. We should elope. We'll start the honeymoon now."

"*Sam.*" She laughed. She couldn't help it. It was a timely reminder of how unsuited they were. Still laughing, she put her hands on his chest and pushed him away. She wanted a man to transport her to the stars, not one who was fifty percent of a comedy act. Especially when she had no intention of auditioning to be the other half of the team. "I'm serious. There's something I really have to tell you."

"Okay," he said, pleased that he'd succeeded in making her laugh. It wasn't as good as kissing her, of course, but there was something so rich and satisfied about her laughter that it ran a close second.

"It's about the thug in the parking lot. I think you might have been right about Moss Whipple. I think he was the person who jumped me."

"What?" He was amused. She was really reaching with that one. It was flattering to see he had her at the point where she couldn't think straight. Moss Whipple, indeed.

She told him about smelling spearmint. "And he was the same size as Moss, too," she said earnestly. "Not especially tall, but chunky, just like Moss." She shuddered as she remembered the bulky arms folding around her, dragging her backward. "The spearmint was the clincher," she said. "Scared as I was, I know I didn't mistake that smell."

"I'm sure you didn't," he soothed, "but I doubt it proves anything."

"Then you don't think it was him?"

"No, it's got to be a coincidence." He smothered a yawn, realizing how tired he was. "Didn't we already go through this routine? The Whipples have no reason to be here. We've got those crooks on our minds for no good reason. It seems to me there are better things we could be thinking about." He lifted himself on an elbow and bent toward her. "Like this, maybe."

He feathered little kisses across her eyelids, then down to an ear. "Mmm. You have the most delicious ears."

"Ears can't be delicious."

"Says who? Confection ears. Yum-yum."

"That's silly. Besides, it tickles."

"It's supposed to. That's part of the recipe."

"What recipe?"

"Old family secret. Can't tell." He was pleased to hear her laugh again, or at least giggle. Here they were, having fun in bed together, he thought with a wry and sleepy smile.

Not exactly the scenario he would have planned, but at least they were together. Smothering another yawn, he rested his head on the pillow and cuddled her close.

After a long, silent moment, Tara realized he was drifting off. She knew it was the time to get up and return to her room, but she delayed. It was best to wait a few more moments. There was no point in rousing him. He might try to give her an argument, and if the argument came in the form of more kisses, she already knew the result. The memory of how he'd made her feel caused her head to spin. It would be best to slip away after she was sure he was soundly asleep.

Sometime later she opened her eyes with an awareness of having fallen asleep herself. Sam's arm lay across her and his knees were tucked up against the back of her legs, his body curved spoon fashion around hers.

She told herself that she had to get up.

"Mmm," Sam murmured drowsily as she stirred. "You feel so good." He nuzzled her shoulder and pulled her more securely into the warm circle of his body as he returned to sleep.

The way she lay in his arms made her feel safe and protected. *In a minute, I'll get up,* she told herself, even while unconsciously nestling more snugly against him. *In just a minute.*

The next thing she knew, sunlight was streaming in through the parted curtains. "Rise and shine, sunshine," Sam called cheerfully.

Smelling coffee, she opened her eyes as Sam placed a tray on the bedside table. He was shaved and dressed and gazing at her warmly.

"What's this?" She lifted herself to a sitting position.

"I went for coffee and croissants. I figured we should have something to eat before leaving for the airport. I tried to let you sleep as late as possible."

She blinked. "Oh, right. The airport." She tried to gather her thoughts. They'd never made definite plans for her to drive him to the airport, but since she was the one with the car, she guessed it had been a foregone conclusion.

"How's your back?"

"Perfect. I had a good nurse." He sat next to her on the bed and adjusted her pillow. "Hey, I forgot to say good-morning, didn't I?" Smiling, he bent forward and kissed her. "A good-morning kiss is even better than words."

Disconcerted, she drew back, then tried to hide her disturbed emotions by taking a sip of coffee. Having a lover bring her breakfast in bed had always seemed the height of romance. But not with him clean scrubbed and tasting of toothpaste while she'd barely awakened. Her fantasies had always gracefully skipped over indelicate details like bleary eyes and morning breath. And she hated knowing that he'd parted the curtains to let the light in while she'd been zonked out, probably sleeping with her mouth open. Yuck.

She belatedly realized she'd been thinking of Sam as her lover. He wasn't, but not because she hadn't given him the opportunity. She watched him with new eyes as he took his coffee and a croissant and moved to a chair. Lingering in his bed all night... who was she kidding? Maybe she *hadn't* ended up staying just because she'd been waiting for him to fall asleep or because she'd fallen asleep herself. Maybe she'd stayed because the physical part of her that had so delighted in dancing close with him felt that his bed was exactly the place to be. It didn't matter that her mind told her he was the wrong kind of man. Being with him had somehow felt *right*.

Then she reminded herself that regardless of her clamoring impulses, she'd called a halt when it counted. Even though she'd stayed with him, she'd never really lost control. Thank goodness. Circumstances had thrown them together and they'd enjoyed some adventures and fun. But no entanglement. And now it was over and everything between them was over, as well. After all, she reasoned, feeling a pang that she immediately dismissed, if he wasn't the man she wanted, why should he feel any differently about her? His ideal woman would be someone like Annette, a person with a zany, happy-go-lucky attitude toward life. Wouldn't it?

Sam finished the last scrap of his croissant, wiped his hand, then checked his watch. "I guess it's getting about time for us to leave."

"Right," she said, getting up, not looking at him. She smoothed her skirt and started hunting for her sandals. It was too bad, she thought with sudden conviction, that Sam didn't have another way to the airport. They really had nothing more to say to each other. There would be no point in planning to get together in the future for "old times' sake." Not that there weren't things about him she might be curious about: did he ever get a line on the stolen ring? Had he finally tracked down the Whipples? Did he win Mr. Dwight-Astor's account? She tried to imagine something about herself that would inspire a similar curiosity on his part. Did being a workaholic pay off? Did she now own the decorator shop? Wow, what cliff-hangers!

She found her sandals half-under the bed. From the corner of an eye, she saw him check his watch again.

"I suppose you'll want to comb your hair and stuff," he said, "but we don't have a whole lot of time. Maybe I shouldn't have let you sleep so late."

Annoyed, she wheeled to face him. "Well, maybe you shouldn't have. You didn't say a word about the time before. I've got to shower and change my clothes."

"You look fine. As I said, maybe you'll want to comb your hair—that's all. You look fine." He didn't understand the fuss. When she came back to the hotel she could take a bath all day if she wanted to. "Your dress is that sort of stuff that looks all wrinkled anyway."

"Not as wrinkled as this, Sam. I *slept* in it."

He grinned. "I guess I should have undressed you. At least partway. Returned the favor, so to speak."

Tara had no idea she could be capable of such instant rage. "I knew you would find some way to bring *that* up." She jammed her feet into her sandals, grabbed her notebook and car keys from the desk and headed for the door.

"Hey, where are you going?"

"To take a shower and get fresh clothes."

He blinked in surprise. "But . . . we really don't have the time. We should be leaving in just a few minutes."

"And I'm not going like this." He should understand— he always looked so bandbox perfect himself. Was his neat appearance and clothes sense simply a natural gift? "I'll need at least half an hour."

He stared at her. Then, never dreaming she would take him up on it, he said, "Then I guess I'll have to take a taxi."

She compressed her lips. "Then I guess you will."

She was outside and in the corridor before he could reply. Hearing a pair of male voices coming from around the corner, she abandoned the idea of the elevator and opted instead for the stairway, which was right next to his room.

The echo of her footsteps was fading on the stairwell as the two men rounded the corner and stopped before Sam's door.

"But what if he hasn't ordered from room service, Elmo?"

"It doesn't matter, Moss," Elmo Whipple answered patiently. "That's just what we say to get in."

"You think she's with him?"

"She's left the cottage—where else could she be? I told you I saw him getting breakfast for two."

Moss chewed thoughtfully on his gum. "That adds up." He hunched his shoulders and assumed a battle stance as Elmo prepared to knock.

Sam was still reeling from Tara's swift departure. After what had happened the previous night or, equally significant, what *hadn't* happened, his plan had been to keep the morning low-key. Tara was a woman who liked things tied up neat and tidy, and he figured that aspect of her personality would start working for him at the airport, when they said goodbye. Wouldn't she start having second thoughts? They'd had some moments when they'd really been good together, and he figured she would start wondering how much better it could have been.

He would make a date to see her back in Philadelphia but keep her guessing about how eager he was. It would leave her unsatisfied, curious. She would keep thinking about him, wondering. Seeing him again would become top priority. He'd been happily nibbling a croissant, dreaming of his big scene at the airport, when he'd suddenly realized he might not be leaving himself enough time. And then, before he knew what was happening, she was as mad as a wet hen and he was supposed to leave for the airport by himself. Where had he gone wrong?

Hearing the knock, Sam hurried to the door, thinking it must be Tara coming back. He opened up and barely had a chance to recognize his callers before Moss had grabbed his arms and bulldozed him backward into the room and up against a wall. His head bounced and he momentarily saw stars. The stars changed into dollar signs. The Whipples were here in Miami. He had a shot at the Bonbon after all.

Elmo closed the door and peered around fretfully. He checked the empty bathroom. "Sit him down, Moss. He's got a question to answer."

"I've got nothing to say to you goons except 'Get out,'" Sam growled, getting over his initial shock and trying to act tougher than he felt. He had no idea why the Whipples had shown up, but maybe they could cut a deal: the Bonbon for whatever they wanted from him.

"Sit him down," Elmo repeated.

Moss shoved Sam into a chair, jamming the sore place on his back. Suppressing the pain, he shrugged free and glowered at Elmo. "So, maybe I've got a question, too."

"Mine, first."

Sam's heart plummeted and all thoughts of a deal flew from his head as he heard Elmo's question: "Where's the girl?"

Tara was in the shower, letting it run hot and hard, regretting how mean she'd been to Sam. She remembered his bewilderment when she'd marched out. But, darn him, it served him right. Where did he get off letting her sleep late, not even mentioning the time, then all of a sudden acting as if it was *her* fault if they took as much as another second?

What an exasperating male. No matter how much she liked him, she sure as heck didn't *want* him. They just didn't make a match. In decorating, she'd seen clients throw good money after bad in the vain attempt to make peace with bad choices. The lesson was even more crucial in life. Know what you want and stick to it. She knew she'd been right in deciding that an association with Sam could come to no good. Where she'd been wrong was in her behavior this morning. She should have made sure they parted as friends.

She dried her hair and dressed, thinking that by that time, his taxi had probably dropped him off at the airport. She imagined him sitting in the departure area, his duffel bag between his knees. He was probably still wondering why she'd turned on him.

Her decision was made in an instant. They shouldn't end things on such a bad note. She would catch him at the airport before his plane left. It was the only right thing to do.

She reached the departure area for the Philadelphia-bound flight in the nick of time. The plane was in, but no one had been allowed to board yet. Out of breath, she anxiously surveyed the waiting passengers. Where was Sam? She saw no one familiar. Maybe he was at a snack bar or in the men's room.

Tara heard the first boarding call. Fidgeting, she stepped out to look up and down the departure concourse. He would surely come running at any minute. The second boarding call came. Where was he? Had he somehow gotten past her?

She waited with growing disbelief as the last passenger filed through the door to the jet way. She hurried to the steward who'd checked the boarding passes, learning that yes, Sam Miller's name had been on the flight list, and no, he hadn't shown up.

An extremely confused Tara was on her way from the terminal when it dawned on her that Sam might not have wanted to part on a bad note, either. While she'd been looking for him at the airport, maybe he'd been back at the hotel looking for her.

She returned to the terminal and the nearest phone. After finding the hotel number in her notebook and dialing, she asked to be connected with Sam's room.

"Hello?" he said.

"Oh, Sam!" The sound of his voice filled her with a rush of glad relief. "Sam—you're there!" Getting a grip on herself, or at least a partial grip, she babbled, "Stay right where you are. I'll be back as soon as I can."

Excited, she hung up and closed her notebook. An unfamiliar envelope slipped out. It was marked with the word Stamps.

Not recognizing the envelope at all, she looked inside. It contained stamps all right, six of them, all in protective shields. She spread them on the telephone shelf. The old-looking stamps pictured an eagle, a ship and several portraits, all printed in blue ink. A half-remembered thought jabbed at her like a broken spring in a Victorian couch. She stared at the blue rectangles. She'd heard something recently about blue stamps...but where? Suddenly it came to her—the Dwight-Astor Blues.

When Sam had explained about the items the Whipples had swiped from the Dwight-Astor safe, he'd mentioned Freddy Dwight-Astor's antique stamps, the individual worth of each stamp heightened by the fact that the collection was all in the same unique shade of blue.

She poked at one of the stamps with a questioning finger. Okay, so maybe they were the Dwight-Astor stamps. But even if they were, how had they gotten in her notebook?

With a stunning burst of realization, the most likely possibility struck: the Whipples had put them there.

Her thoughts tumbled as she fit the picture together. When Sam entered her decorating shop, the Whipples had believed he was a cop. If they'd been carrying the hot stamps, they might have panicked and tried to dump them. Her tote bag, which had contained her notebook, had been in plain sight. Had one of the Whipples shoved the envelope between the notebook pages? Yes, that's what must have happened. And later, when they wanted to retrieve the stamps, they must have learned she'd taken off for Florida. She recalled Annette saying a prospective client had phoned, desperate to know where she was in Florida. It must have been one of the Whipples.

So the Whipples had been in Miami after all! They'd ransacked her room and hired a kid to swipe her purse. It *had* been Moss whom Sam had spotted at the wheel of the white car. Just as it had been Moss who'd tried to grab her in the parking lot.

Breaking out in a fearful sweat, Tara glanced around. She was in a relatively lonely section of the airport, with storage lockers on one side and phone cubicles on the other. Were the Whipples still after her, or had they gotten discouraged?

By now, they had to be convinced that they'd thoroughly searched through everything she had in Miami. They couldn't know the notebook had been with Sam most of the time. It would be logical to think she'd left it at home. Boy, she would like to see them try to search her apartment. Her doorman, Paulie, could take on Godzilla for breakfast and finish off with King Kong as a snack.

Then again, suppose the Whipples had remained in Florida after all?

All of a sudden, she wanted to be back with Sam. This was one time when she was grateful he reminded her of her brothers. Crazy as they were, they were never at a loss. Any action was better than no action—that was their motto. For the moment, she couldn't agree more.

The potential danger of keeping the stamps in her possession hit her as she left the phone. The Whipples had proven they didn't fear risks. Her possessions had been ransacked, she'd been forced into a car chase, mugged.... What might they do next?

She became aware of her panic-stricken breathing and sweaty palms and was suddenly filled with righteous indignation. Why was she, an innocent person, running scared from a pair of hoodlums?

She would keep them from getting their hands on the stamps all right. And then, maybe she would find some way to fix them good.

First the stamps. Calm down, she told herself. Think.

An adage came to mind: the way to catch a crook is to think like a crook. The first thing a criminal would do was stash the loot. She looked at the storage lockers. Wouldn't one of the lockers make a far safer place for the stamps than her notebook?

She hurried to a locker. Presto, change-o! In a flash, the envelope of valuable stamps was gone and in its place was a stout little red locker key. She grinned. All the adventure films she used to watch with her brothers hadn't gone to waste after all.

A few minutes later, with the key safely hidden under the floor mat of her rented car, she started the drive back to the motel and to Sam, feeling proud of herself and ready for just about anything.

Chapter Six

Tara found a parking space almost directly in front of the Fiesta. After making doubly sure the car was safely locked, she shoved the keys into the pocket of her slacks and hurried into the hotel, heading for Sam's room.

"Sam, it's me—Tara," she called out excitedly as she knocked on his door, bursting with eagerness to tell him about the stamps.

The door swung open.

She took a half step inside, then froze. The door had opened seemingly by itself and Sam was seated across the room in a chair—

"Move it, lady," said a voice from behind. She glanced over her shoulder and gasped in horror. A man stood behind her, his face mashed-looking and distorted. Before she could scream, he'd placed his hands on her back. A forceful shove sent her sprawling into the room.

Stumbling, Tara managed to catch herself before she hit the floor. She grabbed the edge of the desk for balance, straightened and turned, her pulse pounding as she confronted the monster. She saw him close the door and realized it was Moss Whipple, a nylon stocking stretched over his face.

"Very smooth, Moss," Elmo Whipple said as he moved from where he'd stood behind the door when he opened it. Then he saw the stocking mask.

"For crying out loud, Moss. What's that on your head?"

"It's my disguise." Moss's words were muffled by the tight-fitting nylon mesh. "I waited in the stairwell for her to come, like you told me to do. I didn't want her to know who I was."

"Jeez! Take it off! All it does is call attention."

"Yeah, but to who?" Moss challenged, his tone making it clear he was convinced he'd won a point.

"Yeah, yeah. Just get it off."

As Moss tore off the mask, Tara, still stunned, turned toward Sam.

"I'm sorry." His smile was weak. He looked dazed and a red mark was on one cheekbone.

She found her voice. "They hurt you!"

"He needed a pop alongside the head," Elmo explained peevishly, moving closer, taking her arm. "He got it for trying to warn you when you called. We said if he got tricky when you showed up, you'd be the one who got popped this time." He steered her toward the other chair. "We've got one quick question, and then—"

"Let go of me," she said indignantly, trying to pull free. "Sam!" Seeking his help, she looked toward him again, which was when she realized he was tied up. It was also the moment when she became fully aware of their predicament.

"Sit," Elmo ordered.

Momentarily cowed, she sat.

"Okay. Where's the notebook?"

"Notebook?" The only thing she could think to do was play dumb.

"The one you had in the store. It was smack in the top of the tote bag. Where is it?"

Looking blank, she stalled, trying to gather her wits. Okay, so she'd walked into a trap, but there must be some way out. "I guess the tote bag must be in my room."

"Not the tote bag," Elmo said with disgust. "The notebook. And don't say it's in your room, because it isn't."

"She's trying to fool us," Moss said, pausing in the task of unwrapping a fresh stick of gum. "I already searched her room real good."

Tara glanced at Sam, whose expression was bleak. No hope there. And he was supposed to be the one with the bright ideas.

"The hotel gave me a *new* room," she said with sudden inspiration, thinking there might be an advantage if she could get one of them to leave. "I'm not in a cottage anymore."

"We found that out," Elmo said. He flicked a thumb in Sam's direction. "*He* tried to tell us you'd checked out and moved to a new hotel, but we found out different."

"And like I said, I searched your room real good," Moss said.

"Oh." The best defense was offense, but nothing came to mind. Lamely, she told Elmo, "If the notebook wasn't in my room, then I guess I must have left it home."

"You didn't." Elmo spoke with certainty.

Suddenly feeling on sure ground, Tara responded with spirit. "What do you have, long-distance X-ray vision? You don't know what's inside my apartment."

"Cousin Gilbert does," Moss volunteered. "He sneaked in last night. He can act like a real gent and knows how to get into places that have alarms and watchmen and fancy stuff. But *I'm* real good at picking locks," he added with obvious pride.

Sam finally had something to say. "That's why they wanted you last night—they thought it would be easier if they could tell Gilbert where to search. And now he's supposed to be coming here."

Oh, great, Tara thought. Sam had finally opened his mouth and the only thing he had to say made her feel even worse. She guessed her best bet was to keep on playing dumb. Nobody knew she'd already found the stamps. Not Sam, not anyone.

She looked at Elmo, blinking innocently. "Why do you want my notebook anyway? There's nothing special about it. Who cares if I can't remember where I put it?"

"It's not the notebook, you stupid broad," Elmo said, losing patience. "It's what's in it. You've got it somewhere and we want it. We searched your room, swiped your purse—" He suddenly focused on the purse she carried. "That's a different one."

Alarmed, Tara hugged her purse close, certain the jig was up. Once they knew she had the notebook, they would guess she'd found what it concealed. Why else would she have kept protesting innocence when she actually had it all the time? *Think,* she ordered herself desperately. *Think.*

Elmo tore the purse free. "Aha!" he cried triumphantly, yanking out the notebook.

"But that's not my *notebook*!" Tara protested. "That's my *address* book." An offensive tactic jumped into her head at last. "I know who you two are! You're rival shop owners! That's why you came into my shop the other day and wrecked it. And now you're after my address list so you can learn the names of my suppliers. Well, let me tell you—"

"Moss!" yelled Elmo, smacking at Tara as she made a grab for the notebook. "Hey, sit her down again."

Moving faster than she would have believed, Moss plunked her back into the chair—hard.

"Now, you sit there," he ordered, his hands resting heavily on her shoulders, "or I'll have to tie you up, too."

"Where are the stamps?" Elmo demanded, who'd turned the notebook upside down and fanned the pages.

Tara stuck to her guns. "I don't know anything about stamps, but I do know you won't get anywhere stealing my list of suppliers. They're extremely loyal, and when they learn what you have in mind, well then—"

"Tara! Tara, calm down," Sam cut in. "This isn't what you think."

"It isn't?" It was about time he put in his two cents. She sure hoped that what he had in mind was good, because she'd just about run dry.

"No, it isn't, so just calm down," he said as if speaking to a child. "Maybe you've been having trouble with some-one trying to steal your customers, but it isn't these two men." Sam addressed Elmo and Moss. "See, I told you characters she didn't know anything about the stamps. She thinks you're business rivals."

"And that's exactly what they are," she insisted hotly, hoping she wasn't pushing her act too far.

"No, no," Sam corrected her, "these men are after the Dwight-Astor Blues. That's a set of valuable stamps that seem to be missing. I explained that the stamps were prob-ably lost during all that commotion in your shop. Like what happened to the glass stones. Your tote bag was probably knocked over."

Tara suddenly realized that was what Sam really believed had happened. She figured she would go along. "Yes, the bag did get knocked over. Everything tumbled out, my n—'' she caught herself in time ''—my address book, everything. The stamps are probably still on the floor of the shop. Unless—'' She sent a startled expression across her face and turned to Elmo. "I bet your stamps got swept up and thrown away. Little stamps in all that mess... Who would have noticed them?''

"She's right about them being awful little,'' Moss offered helpfully.

"They were in an envelope, stupid,'' Elmo snapped.

"They could've dropped out.''

Elmo cursed. "Shut up, Moss, I've got to think.'' He gave Tara a sharp look. "Where were you just now? You went out someplace. Where, to get rid of the stamps?''

She sniffed. "I already said I don't know about your stamps. I...I went out to have my hair done.''

"And it looks very nice, too,'' Sam approved, having decided there might be advantages in keeping Elmo rattled. "I always like it best when you have it done that way.''

She blinked, then picked up on it. "Thank you. I told the beautician that this was your favorite—''

"Shut up, all of you!'' Elmo shouted. He glanced at his watch, then looked at Moss. "What did Gilbert say he was going to do when his plane came in—go to the house in North Dade or meet us here?''

"He never said. He didn't know what plane he would catch.''

"But he knew we were coming here?''

"I told him. But he probably didn't think we would be here this long.''

Elmo digested this a moment, then made his decision. "We'll take this pair to the house and let Gilbert ask the questions. Moss, get the guy up but keep his hands tied.''

"You can't walk a person around with his hands tied,'' Tara objected, hoping to persuade them to free Sam.

"Good point." Elmo pulled a shirt from Sam's duffel bag and tossed it to Moss. "Fasten this around his shoulders so the necktie we used for a rope doesn't show." He grabbed Tara's arm, lifting her from the chair. "Okay now, we're walking to our car in the parking lot. Any funny stuff from either of you and you both get hurt." He gave a meaningful pat to his jacket and Tara saw a bulge that could only mean a gun. "Have you got it?" He looked at Sam, who had seen the meaningful gesture, as well. "Have you got it, too?"

Sam nodded soberly.

As Moss shoved Sam out into the hotel corridor, Sam was busy being disgusted with himself. He owed Tara a carload of apologies, starting with his failure to listen seriously when she talked about Moss the night before. He tried to catch her eye to reassure her, but Elmo was keeping her on his far side. Probably so they couldn't talk and plan an escape.

He tried to think of a likely plan. He had to come up with something before Gilbert, who had a reputation of being more deadly, entered the picture. Three against the two of them would make truly impossible odds. As for the Bonbon, he might as well kiss any hopes of finding it goodbye. The way the Whipples were concentrating on the stamps showed they must have already fenced everything else. Anyway it didn't matter. He had to focus on protecting Tara.

He'd certainly failed her when he'd let the Whipples surprise him that morning. And ditto for later, when he'd tried to sneak the phone off the hook and signal for help and only succeeded in tipping his chair over and knocking himself silly.

He'd still been groggy when Tara arrived. But not so groggy that he hadn't appreciated how well she handled herself. He couldn't help smiling. What a woman. The way she'd buffaloed the Whipples by accusing them of being business rivals had been a stroke of genius. By then, thank God, he'd finally gotten his brain enough in gear to give her a little help.

"What's going on?" Moss questioned, slowing down, yanking Sam's arm to slow him down, as well. A hubbub of voices came from the lobby ahead.

"Just keep moving," Elmo instructed, his tone wary.

Sam's hopes rose. What could be going on at eleven in the morning? Whatever, a distraction might offer a way of escape.

They entered the lobby, finding it filled with guests wearing colorful outfits and carrying cameras. Children chased through a crowd that spilled out to the sun-dappled portico, where a chartered bus stood parked at the curb.

"Tourists going sight-seeing," Elmo muttered. "Just keep on walking."

Sam started moving again, but then he deliberately stumbled, pulling Moss into the edge of the crowd. As he'd hoped, Elmo drifted along with them. Another fake stumble and another sideways pull and the four of them were in the thick of the throng by the time they stepped under the portico. The air was humid and smelled of crushed geraniums, sun lotions and cigar smoke. Sam breathed deeply, never loving a crowd more.

Elmo started to sweat. "Wait up," he told Moss, stopping Tara with a jerk, then irritably shoving her aside as a woman and a youngster jostled against them.

Moss fidgeted. "How'd we get in the middle of this?"

The bus driver opened the door.

"Let's go!" cried one of the children. The crowd surged. Sam realized that Tara now stood beside him. Recognizing his chance when he saw it, he leaned toward her.

"Grab my arm," he ordered, sotto voce.

She gave him a blank look, then his words registered. Unnoticed by Elmo, she linked her arm with Sam's.

"Hold tight," Sam said, and charged forward.

"Hey, wait—" Moss was caught off guard. Elmo was also taken by surprise and Tara slipped free. He hopped to catch up, trying to grab her again.

"Married three days, make way for me and my bride!" Sam bellowed cheerfully as he plowed through the throng with Tara, the two startled crooks in close pursuit. "Here comes the bride!" With good-natured chuckles, people allowed them through. Reaching the bus door, with Tara still clutching his arm, Sam managed to put one foot on the first step and started to climb up behind an elderly couple.

"Oh, no, you don't!" Elmo caught up and yanked Tara's other arm. She cried out but kept her grip on Sam. Dragged back from his perch on the steps, Sam spun to face Elmo.

"What's the matter, buddy?" he asked loudly. "Let the lady in first."

"Yeah, where's your manners?" scolded a bearded man wearing a mouse-ears hat. He shoved Elmo aside. "Let the lady in."

Tara scrambled up the bus steps with Sam at her heels. The woman with the youngster and some others squeezed in next. Sam had counted on the Whipples not getting on the bus, but a glance behind showed him that they had.

"Now what?" Tara asked tensely, having seen them, too.

Sam darted a glance at the bus windows, wishing he and Tara could simply dive out. The windows opened for emergencies, but he couldn't work them with his hands tied. He thought of yelling that the Whipples were crooks, but who would believe him? Besides, there was the gun. With the kids and old people around, somebody innocent was bound to get hurt.

Incoming passengers kept them shuffling along. He heard the child behind him whine, "But I *do*, Mommy. I got to go potty."

Was there a window in the rest room? Sam figured there must be.

"The rest room," he told Tara. "We're going to lock ourselves in."

Wriggling past passengers who were taking their seats, Tara and Sam hurried down the narrow aisle and crammed into the rest room. Tara, who had gone in first, darted a hand around Sam to latch the door. For a moment he panicked, not seeing a window. Then he located it, the glass opaque to provide privacy.

"My hands—" Elbows inadvertently brushing Tara's breasts, he shoehorned his body around in the narrow space so she could reach the necktie knotted about his wrists. She flipped his dangling shirt out of the way and had the knot nearly undone when the door rattled.

"The door's stuck, Mommy," piped the child.

Elmo's angry voice came next, followed by hard thumps on the door. "You wait your turn!" cried the indignant mother. "Can't you see the child was here first?"

Sam's hands were free. Flexing his arms, he pivoted in the cramped space, his hip pushing against Tara's thigh as he crouched to release the window lever. He shoved the loosened panel and grunted in triumph as it swung outward. Daylight poured in.

The angry racket continued on the other side of the door as Sam threw his leg over the window's rim. Breathing hard, he estimated the drop to the ground. He took another breath, then scrambled the rest of the way out and turned to drop down. He let go and his feet hit the paving, his second shirt billowing like a superhero's cape. Tara was already halfway out the window. Her slacks pulled taut against her rounded bottom as she swung her feet down. He reached up to assist her. "It's okay, just let go—I've got you." She released her grip and dropped into his arms, pressing against him as she slid to the ground.

"They're on to us," she said with a gasp as she looked up to see the enraged face of Elmo Whipple at a bus window. "Let's go." She yanked the car keys from her pocket. "I'm parked behind the bus."

A moment later, they were in the little yellow sedan with Tara in the driver's seat. A delivery van had parked close behind, boxing them in.

Sam rolled down the car window and stuck his head out to see how much room she had to back up. He looked up and saw Elmo and Moss on the sidewalk outside the bus. "Don't look now, but here come the Whipples."

As Tara reversed, Sam saw a third man join them. Elmo and Moss gestured wildly, pointing out the car.

"Cousin Gilbert," Sam muttered, recognizing the sharp-featured man from a mug shot he'd seen back in Philadelphia. "Step on it, Tara!"

As the three Whipples stampeded toward them, Tara cleared the van and spun the wheel, pulling the car out of the spot.

Gilbert Whipple made a flying leap. One of his hands raked the sill of the open car window. Tara stomped on the accelerator and they tore off, leaving Gilbert behind in the dust.

Sam sagged in his seat, feeling in a state of shock. There had been no mistaking the ring Gilbert had been wearing—the Bonbon Ring.

"Are they following?" Tara asked, glancing at a yellow traffic light. She normally slowed for yellow lights, but this time she speeded up and darted through the intersection as the signal turned red.

She realized she'd never felt better in her life. She'd nearly run a red light and it somehow felt terrific. Flushed with enthusiasm, she glanced over at Sam, whose attention was on the back window. What a team they made! There was no one close behind them and she took the next corner without flipping her turn signals. She was really in the groove now. Let those hooligans try to follow her. Just let 'em try.

"Sam—" She cut the next corner and zoomed around a wide curve. "Moss had a white car the night we chased him. Do you see it anywhere?"

"The way you're driving, I can hardly see anything." He'd grabbed for his seat belt as he spoke and was putting it on. The way she'd taken that last corner! The poor kid was a bundle of nerves. Captured, roughed up... it was no wonder she was badly shaken. He unfastened the shirt the Whipples had used to hide his hands and tossed it into the back seat. He saw that they were now on Indian Creek Drive.

"You can slow down," he cautioned, and was relieved when she did so. "Elmo said they were parked in the hotel lot. By the time they get on the road, they'll have no idea where to hunt for us." He turned to look behind them again, then started rolling up the window. "No idea at all."

Tara frowned at him. "So where's the big hooray? The all-right-a-rooney, shazam, we sure got away from those suckers?"

He blinked. "What do you mean?"

"Sam, we made it. The Big Escape. We were splendid. *Magnificent.* And now you've got a face like somebody stole your ice cream cone."

"Oh." He hadn't realized his mixed emotions showed. "It's because I saw Gilbert wearing the Bonbon Ring."

Tara's eyes lit up. "But that's wonderful! When the Whipples get caught—and if I have anything to say, they *will* get caught—the ring has been saved. Your Mr. Dwight-Astor will be delighted. It's worked out perfectly!''

Startled, Sam realized it had been nerve rather than nerves that had accounted for Tara's reckless driving. She'd actually been *enjoying* herself. Seeing her cut loose was exactly what he'd thought would be so good for her—although not necessarily behind the wheel of a car. He hated to throw cold water on her enthusiasm, but he had no choice.

"It hasn't worked out at all. I'm supposed to get the ring back in a way that won't let Mrs. Dwight-Astor know it was ever missing in the first place."

Tara's face fell. "That's right, I forgot. She believes her husband has it stored safely in the bank vault."

Sam nodded morosely. "I'd more or less resigned myself to the fact that the ring was gone. The important thing was to get you away from the Whipples. Then Gilbert appeared and literally shoved the ring under my nose."

"So what's so bad about that?"

"Because the important thing is your safety. In fact, we should head for the airport right now. Take the next causeway across the bay and we'll head for Miami International. You've got to get out of here. As long as the Whipples have the goofy notion that you know something about the Dwight-Astor Blues—"

Tara's laugh interrupted him. "But I do know about them. More than that—I *have* them."

"You what?"

"I have them. Or at least, I know where they are." Instead of taking the causeway as Sam had suggested, Tara swung off to the north again, going slowly along residential streets as she talked, telling Sam how she'd found the stamps and hidden them.

"The locker key is right here in the car," she concluded. "Under the floor mat."

Sam fished under the mat and found the key. He placed it on his knee and stared at it. He looked from the key to Tara. "I'm impressed," he said, slowly. "Truly impressed." He started to laugh. "Tara, you're wonderful. A woman in a thousand."

"Thank you." She glowed. "I'm glad you're looking more cheerful. Even if you never get the Bonbon, Mr. Dwight-Astor will be awfully pleased with you for rescuing the stamps."

"No, no," he said, seeing the possibilities. "The stamps are the answer to my prayers. I'll use them to bargain for the ring."

Her eyebrows drew together. "Is that wise? With all the trouble the Whipples are going to, the stamps must be worth a lot. And they're a sure thing. If you try to make a deal, you risk losing the stamps *and* the ring. Mr. Dwight-Astor might be glad to settle for the stamps."

Sam thought for a moment. He was sure Freddy would put the ring ahead of anything else, but then again, Tara had a point. "The stamps probably *are* worth more than the ring," he admitted, "but I don't think that's what will count with Freddy. I'll need a fast phone call to him to make certain."

"What we also need," Tara said in a worried tone as she looked at the dashboard, "is gasoline. The needle's on empty. I don't know how long it's been that way. I've never run out of gas in my life."

Sam was amused. She sounded more disturbed by the idea that she'd allowed something uncharacteristic to happen than she was by the event itself.

"I see a station in the next block," he said, then he thought of something that momentarily erased his smile. "The Whipples took my wallet. And your purse is in my room. Do you have any money?"

"No. You don't have anything?"

He shook his head. "They even cleaned out my change."

Tara clenched her hands around the steering wheel. "You mean we're stranded?"

His confidence returned. "Not by a long shot. Pull into the station up ahead and park past the pumps. I'll ask where I can find a phone. I'll make sure Freddy still wants me to go after the Bonbon."

"But we don't have money for the call."

"I use my phone credit card often enough to know the number. And I'll ask Freddy to forward us cash through a Miami branch of one of his banks."

Tara switched off the ignition as Sam got out. She wondered if there would be enough fuel to start up again. The exuberant high she'd felt when they'd been on the move had faded. She knew why she hadn't kept her usual eye on the gas gauge. She'd gone tearing to the airport after Sam, then made a beeline back, thinking of nothing except the stamps. And him.

She'd been imagining how excited he would be. Thinking how pleased he would be when he learned how she'd helped him out.

Sam returned almost immediately. "The attendant thinks there's a pay phone in that gift shop across the street. Lock the car and come on. We might as well both go."

They crossed the street and entered the shop, which was jammed with Florida souvenirs, trinkets and novelties. A harried-looking woman was behind the counter, unpacking boxes.

"On the back wall," she said in answer to Sam's inquiry about the phone. "But you may not have much luck. Most likely all you'll hear are crackles and static—somebody's supposed to come look at it. If you can't get through, you'll have to try the booth on the corner."

Sam thanked her and turned to Tara. "We might as well check it out since we're here."

They went past shelves of party items, ceramics and novelties made of shark's teeth and seashells. They were almost to the back of the shop when he stopped, his attention caught by a display of stuffed caiman lizards, the baby alligator look-alikes dressed in celebrity costumes. "Hey, look at these." Grinning, he pointed out a blond-wigged reptile in a corsetlike top, leather skirt and miniature junk jewelry. "It's supposed to be Madonna. Kind of cute, huh?" He looked at Tara in time to catch her rolling her eyes.

"There's the phone," she said. "And I hope we can find a drinking fountain. I'm thirsty."

"Right." He felt miffed. Okay, so stuffed lizards were tacky. Did that mean a person couldn't get a kick out of seeing one gussied up like a rock star? Tara was a class act and he loved that quality about her, but sometimes she went overboard.

"Now that you mention it," he told her, "I'm thirsty, too. While I'm on the phone, check the floor for dropped change. Maybe you can treat me to a soda."

Let her roll her eyes over *that*, he thought with a grin as he scooted off.

The phone was as bad as the woman behind the counter had warned. Unable to get through, Sam hung up and went back to find Tara. She wasn't where he'd left her, but he found her in a far corner of the shop, smiling and talking to an elderly, white-haired man. As Sam approached them he had the opportunity to appreciate the picture she made, the smooth lines of her fair hair curving about her lovely, fine-boned face, her body slim, yet delectably feminine under her tailored, light-colored slacks and cream-white shirt, the long sleeves casually folded up.

The white-haired man nodded to Sam, tipped his cap to Tara and moved on.

"Oh, boy," Sam said, teasing. "Turn my back for a second and you're after a new guy."

She gave him a deadpan look. "The floor was clean so I was trying to bum some change."

Sam's eyes bugged. "What?" She giggled and he realized that he'd been had.

"You should see your expression!" She was still giggling. "Actually, the man was really hunting for the birthday candles and he mistook me for a clerk. I told him I wasn't one but I was able to point the candles out anyway. Did the phone work?"

"Thank goodness it didn't." Sam shook his head. "No telling what you would have dreamed up if I'd been away any longer." *What a delight she is.* Sam wondered if it would always be that way. He took her arm and was aware of her softness, her warmth. His pockets might be empty, but simply touching her made him feel as though he had a million bucks. "I guess we're in for a hike to that phone booth—"

He stopped as if turned to stone. Tara followed his gaze through the glass of the display window and on across the street. The three Whipples stood in the gas station lot, peering at the yellow sedan.

Tara gasped and drew back, bumping against a display of plaster flamingos. "How could they follow us? You said that by the time they got their car out, our trail would be cold."

The reappearance of the crooks made Sam feel as if he'd been punched. "Gilbert must have been parked near enough to the bus to get going right away. I didn't see anyone following, but I didn't keep looking. I was so sure we'd gotten away clean."

He looked out the window again and his spirits lifted a fraction. "I bet they've got no idea where we've gone. Maybe they lost us at the last turn and cruised around until they saw the car."

Tara got up her courage to peek out. "It looks as if they're going to the station. As soon as they step inside, we'd better run for it."

"No, it's too open out there. They'd spot us before we got anywhere." He cast a frantic look around and saw the white-haired man heading for the door.

Sam grabbed Tara's hand and caught up with the man. "Excuse me, but if you're on your way out and have a car, could you possibly give my friend and me a lift? We've had some engine trouble."

The man shifted his sack of purchases to his other arm. "I reckon I might." He pushed his cap back thoughtfully. "Lift to where?"

Sam thought fast. All he wanted was to get away from where they were, but he couldn't say that. The man looked local—he probably wasn't going any great distance. "To the nearest major road would be fine. We could pick up another ride from there."

The white-haired man studied them.

Standing with her hand squeezed tightly in Sam's, Tara realized she was holding her breath. Had the Whipples already entered the gas station? The attendant would remember directing Sam across the street. It wouldn't be long before the Whipples were crossing the street, too. If the white-haired man was going to say no, she wished he would say it in a hurry, because otherwise they were only wasting time—

"Know anything about dogs?" the man asked abruptly. "Do you like 'em?"

"Sure I like dogs," Sam answered quickly. Tara was too surprised to say anything at all.

"How about the lady?"

Tara felt Sam give her a poke. "Yes, yes," she said. "I like dogs. *Love* dogs." She hoped she'd given the right answer. Apparently she had, for the man beamed.

"Then we've got a deal. I'll take you wherever you want to go after you two give me some help. It shouldn't take us long—it's just a short distance. I'm picking out a puppy as a present for my granddaughter. I could use some shared opinions."

Chapter Seven

They piled into the man's enclosed Jeep—Tara in the front, Sam in the back. They were just pulling into traffic when the Whipples, talking and gesturing, emerged from the gas station. Elmo ducked around the corner of the building—probably to keep a watch on the car from hiding. Gilbert's gaze moved toward the street and both Tara and Sam scrunched down. By the time they straightened and dared look back, they could no longer see the Whipples and had no idea if they'd been spotted or not.

"You okay?" The white-haired man asked, giving Tara a puzzled glance.

"Just fine," she answered brightly, rubbing her neck and swiveling her head in an exaggerated fashion. If the man guessed they were being chased, he might want to dump them. "Just trying to work a crick out of my neck."

"She gets them a lot," Sam said, leaning forward to massage her neck and shoulders. "How's that feel, honey?"

"Thanks, that's a lot better." Pretending to look around and thank Sam gave her another chance to look out the back window and hunt for the Whipples. She didn't see their car and Sam's shrug told her he hadn't seen them, either.

"We really appreciate you helping us out," Sam told the man as Tara faced front again.

Their savior was Loomis Perkins, retired from the army. "Folks call me Captain," he said with a cackling laugh, "but that's showing a hell of a lot more respect for this white hair than it is for the truth. Now, what happened to your car?"

It had occurred to Sam that if Freddy Dwight-Astor sent him money, he would need identification to claim it. The Whipples had lifted his cash but had left his cards in his wallet, which was still in his room. So what he wanted to do was get back to the hotel.

"It broke down when we were on our way to meet friends at a hotel called the Fiesta," he said. "Maybe you've heard of it? It's a nice place directly on the beach."

Captain Perkins nodded cheerfully. "Sure, I know which one it is. As soon as we finish looking over the puppies, I'll drive you there."

"That would be great," Sam said.

Tara spoke up. "What pretty scenery we're passing through." She used an interest in the sights as an excuse to look for the Whipples again. "These houses are painted such pretty pastel shades. And the colors of those shrubs! They have leaves as bright as parrots." She turned to give Sam an anxious stare. "Have you seen any of those special shrubs, Sam?"

"No, I haven't."

"They're awfully interesting. You'd better keep looking."

"I will. Don't worry."

Noticing the captain giving her a funny glance, Tara decided she ought to cool it. Let Sam do the Whipple hunting
from the back seat, where it wouldn't be so obvious. She
hugged her arms about herself. The afternoon was warm,
but nervousness made her skin feel chilled and clammy. She
still hadn't gotten over the shock she'd felt when she'd
looked out the gift shop window and saw the crooks.

"How much farther is it to the puppies?" she asked the
captain after they'd driven over a causeway and were in
Miami proper.

"Only a few more miles."

"Are we going to a breeder's?" She found it a struggle to
keep her voice sounding normal.

The captain chuckled. "Nothing as fancy as that. My
friend Madge has a litter she's looking to give away. The
pups are mongrels, but the mother dog looks sort of like
Lassie. You know, the collie that had her own TV show?
Seems like that sort of dog will make a good-natured pet for
an eight-year-old."

"That's what your granddaughter is? Eight years old?"
Tara chattered without paying attention to her words. "A
collie puppy sounds really nice." As she and the captain
talked, she kept sneaking glances in the side mirror, trying
to check the traffic behind them.

They drove a mile or two in silence, then the captain asked
abruptly, "Miss, are you sure everything's all right?

"All right?" Tara widened her eyes innocently. "Sure,
everything's fine. Why shouldn't it be?"

The man frowned. "Well, I couldn't help noticing the pair
of you act jumpy, and there's been this car—"

"What car?" Tara and Sam asked in unison. Tara felt as
if her heart had leaped into her throat. "You mean a white
car?"

"A light-colored car, yes." He eyed his rearview mirror. "I don't see it right now, but putting it together with how you two have been acting, I couldn't help thinking that somebody might be following you."

Tara and Sam exchanged glances. Tara was thinking that they had no idea what kind of vehicle Gilbert had. Even if the car the captain thought he saw following wasn't white, it could still be the Whipples.

"I've been having problems with my ex-boyfriend," she said, making up something fast. "He and his buddies have been following me places, making nuisances of themselves." She tried to sound exasperated rather than alarmed.

The old man cackled. "Thought it might be something like that. The way you two kept looking out the window and all. Want me to try and lose them?"

"Could you do that?" Sam asked eagerly.

"I sure could try, sonny."

"That would be great!"

"There they are again," the captain announced. "Don't look! I know how it goes on those TV chase shows. We don't want to let them know we're on to them." He sounded as if he was having the time of his life.

"Are they catching up?" Tara asked, her voice unsteady. She'd scrunched down in her seat again.

"No, they just seem to be hanging back there about a block and a half behind. Tell you what I think we should do. I'll pull into the next side street and stop halfway down. You two hop out and cut through the yards until you see a pink house with a high fence. That's where the puppies are. You knock on the door and tell Madge that Captain Perkins told you to wait there for him."

"What are you going to do in the meantime?" Sam asked.

"I'll lead that boyfriend a merry chase, then come back and park in front of Madge's house. If I haven't been able to shake him, when I get out and leave an empty Jeep, he still won't know where I left you two off. For all he'll know, it could have been miles away."

Tara laughed in relief. "Captain, that sounds wonderful."

The old man beamed. "Can't have anybody spoiling the day for a nice young couple like you. He'll go looking for you someplace else and be miles on the wrong track by the time we get done with the puppies and are on the road again."

Their plan agreed upon, the man turned down the side street. Tara and Sam flung themselves out and scrambled to hide behind thick bushes as the Jeep pulled away. They kept themselves flat and waited until there were no sounds of traffic before they stood up again.

"Several cars drove past," Tara said, brushing twigs and leaves from her clothes. "Did you see them?"

"No, I was afraid they might see us if I looked at the wrong time."

"Me, too." She cast an anxious look at the side street, which had fallen quiet. "Maybe it wasn't them, or maybe we lost them when the Jeep turned down here."

Sam bit his lip. "Whatever, I can't see that they'd have any idea where we are now." He reached for her hand. "Come on, let's find the pink house and wait for the captain."

They found the house without any trouble. A gray-haired woman appeared at the side door when they knocked.

"You're helping the captain pick out a puppy?" she asked, when they'd explained. "Well, isn't that nice. The litter is right here, inside the yard." She unlatched the squeaky gate and escorted them inside the enclosure. The puppies came running.

"Four of them!" cried Tara. "No, five!" By the time Madge had led them over to the shrubby saw palmetto which screened the doghouse, five pups were clustered around their feet. Tara laughed, feeling relief. Being behind the tall fence made her feel almost safe for the first time since they'd fled the gift shop.

Madge introduced them to the mother dog, who did indeed resemble Lassie. After giving them a thorough sniffing and a few thoughtful woofs, the old dog lolled back under a Norfolk pine, accepting them as friends.

Three of the litter were the tan-and-white of the mother, with pointed faces and the fluffy coats of collies. Of the two remaining, one was all black with a smooth coat and the other was black-and-white. Sam scooped up the black one.

"Bet your father was a black Labrador," he told the wriggling bundle. The answer he got was an enthusiastic face licking.

With a smile, Madge said, "I'm going to finish up some work I was doing in the house. You two look over the puppies, and when the captain arrives, I'll tell him you're already waiting here in the back."

"Oh, Sam," Tara said after Madge left. "They're so cute, aren't they? I wish we had time to enjoy them." She bent to lift a pup into her arms, lost her balance and plunked down on her bottom. She giggled as the puppies scrambled over her, all squeals and little paws, wet noses and warm wet tongues.

Sam knelt down, too, his eyes sparkling with pleasure at the picture Tara made. She shook her hair back and smiled at him, holding a pup for his inspection. "Isn't this one adorable?"

"It sure is. What we should do is decide on one of them. As soon as the captain shows up, we'll show him the one we like and maybe that will speed things up. I want to get back to the hotel as soon as possible."

"Okay. I was surprised when you told him we wanted to go there. I figured your first thought would be to find a phone and call Mr. Dwight-Astor."

Rolling one of the pups around, letting it bite his finger, Sam explained about needing his identification.

"But if we go back to the hotel, you won't need to ask Mr. Dwight-Astor to send you money," Tara pointed out. "The Whipples didn't touch anything in my purse besides my notebook. I have cash as well as traveler's checks."

Sam shook his head. "I'm not borrowing from you—at least, not for anything more than taxi fare to the airport. If I have to tangle with the Whipples again, I don't want you anywhere around." His tone became even more emphatic. "Other than picking up my wallet, I'm not doing anything else until I see you safely out of Miami. I can call Freddy after I see your plane off."

Tara's eyes narrowed. "I'm afraid you've got the cart before the horse, Sam. I'm not going anywhere until I know whether or not you're fool enough to go up against three crooks and a gun."

Sam frowned. "We can hash that out later."

A noise came from the house. Startled, Sam and Tara peered anxiously around the bushes. They saw the captain had opened a window and was leaning out. "I'll join you in a minute or two," he called.

"That was quick," Sam called back. "How did things go?"

"No problem." The elderly man lifted a hand and put his thumb and forefinger together in an okay signal. He shut the window.

Sam grinned at Tara. "Guess that means your 'old boy-friend' is out of the picture." His gaze was admiring. "It was terrific when you made up that story. Maybe the Whipples were never following anyway, but it sure perked up the captain. I bet he hasn't had so much fun in years."

Tara blushed at his praise. "I just tried to think of some-thing that wouldn't sound alarming."

"You did good." He lifted the pup he'd been playing with. "Let's pick this one. I want to be ready as soon as he comes out."

While waiting for the captain, Tara noticed that the mother dog was starting to act nervous. She gave a restless woof and lifted herself to her haunches. A low, rumbling sound started from deep in her throat.

"She's getting tired of us playing with her pups," Tara said, setting down the little dog she'd been holding.

"I don't think we're the trouble. She's not even looking our way." Sam followed the collie's gaze, which was trained on the fence. "It sounds as if there's somebody in the yard next door."

Tara frowned. "If it's just the people next door, you'd think she'd be used to them." She heard a bumping sound, as if something was being dragged, then a solid thump on the other side of the fence. She also thought she heard a muffled curse, but she couldn't be positive because the dog was still growling. Feeling uneasy, she wished she had some way of seeing through to the other yard.

"I don't like this," she said, her uneasiness growing. She started to get up.

The collie suddenly leaped to her feet and began a fu-rious, ringing bark.

"All right! All right!" Tara cried, frightened, sitting down again, thinking the dog was barking at her. Then she saw the dog frantically jumping up and down and staring overhead. Tara looked up, too. An oak tree stood in the yard next door, long branches stretching out over the fence. Moss Whipple had suddenly appeared in the tree. Red-faced from exertion, he was scrambling to lift himself onto a higher branch.

Tara yelped and grabbed Sam's sleeve, pointing wildly.

Sam stared in amazement.

Seeing that he'd been spotted, Moss tried to give them a menacing look while struggling to heave himself higher. A cluster of twigs was in his way, keeping him from getting his knee up. Sam couldn't imagine what Moss thought he was going to do from the tree and he didn't care. All he knew was that they'd been followed after all. Jumping to his feet, one of the pups still tucked under his arm, he scooped up a dog's water dish and heaved it toward the crook.

Moss dodged and fought for his balance as the dish bounced off the tree trunk. He slipped and dangled awkwardly, his trousers caught on a branch. An angry shout came from below as the dish clattered down.

Hardly able to hear himself over the dog's continued barking, Sam yelled for Tara to follow him. With the forgotten pup tucked under his arm like a football, he led her toward the gate just as Madge and the captain came out to see why the dog was making such a fuss.

"The ex-boyfriend—" Sam said by way of explanation as he galloped by them. "Followed us after all. Tree next door..." From behind him, he heard Moss yelling. It sounded as if he might be stuck. Sam sincerely hoped he was. He pulled Tara through the gate and was starting to slam it when Madge called, "Wait! Where are you going with that puppy?"

Sam looked dumbfounded at the black puppy that he still held. He dashed back and breathlessly thrust it into the captain's arms. "This is the one we like the best. Thanks for everything. We've got to go!"

Dragging Tara across the grass, he led the way through the yards, back the way they'd come in the first place. Hearts pounding, they darted through a well-watered section of new lawn, almost slipping in the mud. That was all they needed now, Sam thought, a fall and a turned ankle. They didn't look back until they reached the bushes where they'd hidden when they first jumped out of the Jeep. Eyes wide, they searched the empty yards behind them. There was no sign of anyone in pursuit. They looked over the roof of an intervening house and could see only the top of the oak tree. The collie still barked hysterically in the distance and it sounded as if Moss was yelling for help.

"The Whipples must still be there," Tara gasped, her lungs burning.

"At least it sounds as if Moss is." Sam cast a frenzied glance around, wondering what they should do next. "There's no way of telling where Gilbert and Elmo are. Maybe they left Moss stuck in the tree and now they're hunting for us."

As they stood behind the bushes trying to catch their breath, an aging pickup truck rode past, heading toward the main street. The truck's tailgate was missing and there were flat crates tied down in the back with a tarp. The truck windows were open and the radio played a lively Cuban song. The truck slowed as the driver prepared to stop at the corner.

Sam tugged Tara's hand. "Time to hitch another ride."

They had no problem scrambling aboard the truck, but there was no room for them except on either side of the lashed crates. Sam signaled that they lie down flat. Tara, who needed no cuing, was already doing exactly that, threading her fingers under a section of the tarp and through the slats of the crate for something to hold on to. The driver, singing loudly along with the music, gave no indication he was aware he'd taken on passengers. He put his foot on the gas. The crates banged together, making odd noises as the truck pulled out into the street.

Something tickled Tara's nose. She sneezed. She felt a sharp sensation on her knuckle and jerked her hand from the crate, not sure what had poked her. There was an odor she didn't like, but she was in no mood to complain. She had her eyes squeezed shut and realized she was childishly pretending that as long as she couldn't see anyone, nobody could see her. Opening her eyes, she looked down along her feet and out the open end of the jouncing truck. They passed Madge's house and she saw the Jeep parked by the curb. There was no sign of the Whipples and she figured they were still trying to get Moss down from the tree.

She heaved a sigh of relief and got another whiff of the unpleasant odor. What had they landed themselves in, a garbage truck? She would have liked to sit up, but she was afraid of being spotted. She tried to look over to Sam, but the tarp-covered crate was in her line of vision. One corner of the tarp had slipped and had started to flap in the breeze, exposing the end of the crate. She angled uncomfortably about, figuring she could look through the slats and see Sam on the other side. Cold beady eyes stared at her. She gasped and jerked back and sneezed again as more feathers floated by. *Chickens.* The crates in the pickup truck were filled with chickens.

The truck took them back into Miami Beach, going over a different causeway than the one the captain had taken earlier. Stiff and cramped from the bouncing ride, she saw with relief that they'd arrived in the section where tall luxury hotels loomed on both sides of the street.

"Let's get out!" Sam hollered through the chicken crate. The chickens squawked angrily and tried to attack him. That was nothing new. Every time the truck had stopped or started, he and Tara had grabbed the rails of the crates to steady themselves and their reward had been angry chickens and pecked fingers.

Tara shouted enthusiastic agreement with bailing out. When the truck stopped for the next light, they climbed out, going over the sides instead of the back. The driver saw them. He shouted, demanding to know what they thought they were doing, but by that time, the light had changed and horns were blowing for the truck to move on.

"The worst ride of my life, but thank God for it," Tara gasped, standing on the curb, brushing at her clothes and hair. "Did I get all the feathers off?"

Sam, who'd been brushing his own clothes and hair, gave attention to hers. "Almost." He tweaked away stray fluffs that were caught on the inside of her collar. It looked as if there was another one down the neck of her blouse. He was thinking it might be interesting to go on a determined search for stray feathers, but there was no time for that now.

He glanced around. "We have our bad luck, but we have our good luck, too. We're only a few blocks from the hotel."

"That's what I was hoping," Tara said, also hoping she didn't smell like chickens. She gave an uneasy look at the passing traffic. "I keep expecting the Whipples to pop up at any moment, like jack-in-the-boxes."

"I know what you mean." Sam took her hand as they started hurrying toward the Fiesta. "As dumb as they are, they had a few tricks up their sleeves after all."

Chapter Eight

They hurried along the street, Sam busy thinking that not only did he want to get back to the hotel fast, he also wanted to get on their way to the airport. He wondered if Tara was going to give him a hard time about leaving. Back in the dog yard, before the Whipples had shown up, she'd said something that made him afraid she might.

Tara was busy with her own concerns. Why couldn't Sam see the wisdom of going to the police? She imagined uniformed men in a police car, chasing the crooks down, jumping out and handcuffing them. Elmo's worried face would look more worried than ever and Gilbert would probably be yelling for his lawyer. Before the police put Moss in their car, they would probably make him spit out his gum. She smiled in satisfaction at the thought. Now, if she could only convince Sam to see things her way.

"Here we are," he said, taking her arm as they arrived at the hotel. He escorted her inside, remembering all too vividly what had happened in the lobby that morning. "You're awfully quiet," he said, hoping she was also remembering their narrow escape and was mentally packing her bags for her flight home, but no such luck.

"I've been imagining seeing the Whipples in jail. And that's what you should be thinking about, too. Doesn't the way they treated you make you furious?"

"Sure it does." What was she saying—that he acted as if it didn't bother him? He didn't know what she was driving at.

"Being tied up with your own necktie?"

"Of course it makes me mad. Damned mad." He guided her around a linen cart of housekeeping paraphernalia and cleaning supplies that sat unattended by the elevator door.

"Then if you're really fed up with the way the Whipples acted, you should do something about it." She spoke with heat. "Trading the stamps for the Bonbon isn't getting justice. But if we turn them over to the police, we get the ring back *and* keep the stamps. In the long run, wouldn't that be better for everyone? Even Mrs. Dwight-Astor would see that."

"I don't know why we're discussing this," Sam said, not slackening his pace. "I said I'd find out if Freddy still wants the ring. And if he still wants it, I'm game to go after it." He rounded the corner and was almost to his door when he came to an abrupt halt.

"I can't believe I've been so stupid," he muttered, staring at his door with the kind of alarm usually reserved for locked attic rooms in horror films. Before Tara could ask what was wrong, he grabbed her arm and pulled her past his room and into the stairwell, going up a step so they were hidden from the corridor.

In a low voice, he said to her, "Suppose the Whipples have somehow beaten us back here?"

"You mean you think they might be waiting in your room?"

"Where would be a better place? With the way Moss can pick locks, it would be a cinch."

"You're too much," she snapped, annoyed. "You're all bent out of shape because they might be in your room, but you don't have a second's hesitation about going up against them for the Bonbon. What kind of sense does that make?"

"All kinds of sense. When I make a deal for the ring, you won't be along. It's your safety I'm worried about, not mine."

"The Whipples may be tricky," Tara said, "but they're not here. At least not yet. Remember what happened this morning? Moss waited right here in this stairwell so he could come from behind and shove me inside when the door opened. If they were here, this is where Moss would be."

Sam saw her logic. "You're right. That numskull would figure if something worked once, it would work twice." He drew his brows together. "Even so, I don't want to open my room until I'm absolutely sure."

Tara's eyes suddenly glowed. "I've got an idea."

With a puzzled Sam at her heels, she retraced their steps back to the linen cart in front of the elevator. She took up a dark blue cleaning staff smock and slipped it on, then draped a towel over her head and gave it a twist to secure it. It wasn't the sort of arrangement that would stay in place for long without a pin, but it would do for the time she needed. She lifted a tall stack of towels and faced Sam. At a casual glance, she appeared to be a different person than the one she'd been only a moment before.

"Excuse me, sir," she said softly, stepping past Sam as if she didn't know him.

Understanding, Sam saw the brilliance of her plan. She would go to the door masquerading as a member of the housecleaning staff. If the Whipples didn't respond, she could unlock the door, still pretending to be a maid. If the Whipples were inside, there would be an instant when they would view Tara as a stranger. It would give her a chance to back off and he would jump in swinging, giving her a chance to get away. It was a hell of a lot better than walking smack into a trap. And it would help even more if he had some sort of weapon. A dry mop was leaning against the cart and he grabbed it up. Anything was better than nothing.

At his door, Tara lifted an eyebrow in question. He nodded, mop in one hand, key held ready in the other. Everything should happen fast to keep the element of surprise.

"Maid service," she called loudly. There was no sound from inside and Sam quickly unlocked the door. He shoved it open and stepped aside.

There was a frozen moment. "Nobody's home," Tara announced, her voice high-pitched with tension.

"We'll make sure." Sam rushed in, holding the mop in both hands. The closet stood open and nobody was hidden behind the door. He charged into the bathroom and drove the mop handle through the drawn shower curtain and swung it from side to side. *Take that…and that!* There was nobody there to take anything. He gave a gusty sigh of relief, then hurried from the bathroom.

"Did you lock the door?" he asked Tara.

"Yes." She'd taken off the smock and towel and was picking up her purse from the floor. She straightened and looked around, edgy nervousness in her gesture. "The door's locked, but now I feel trapped. Like somebody's going to start picking the lock any second."

The thought seemed to grip his stomach. "Maybe they will." He snatched up his wallet. "Come on, let's get out of here."

They made sure the hallway was clear, then hurried out. Around the corner, he said, "You don't have anything you really need from your room, do you? It's too risky to fool around here. I can pack your stuff later and bring it back to Philadelphia for you."

She realized he was proceeding with the idea that she would leave Miami as soon as possible. This wasn't the place to argue. "There's nothing I can't live without."

"Okay, let's make tracks." As they hurried along the corridor, he said, "We'd better not go out to the street right in front of the hotel. We'll leave by the beach side. We can walk along the water for a few blocks and cut through some other hotel."

They went through the lobby as rapidly as possible without calling attention to themselves, and kept up the pace as they passed through the garden and the pool area.

"This is only the second time I've been on the beach," Tara said, out of breath as they left the terrace and started across the sand. The fresh salt air smelled wonderful to her heaving lungs.

"It hasn't been much of a vacation, has it?" Sam was thinking that if he hadn't come into her shop, the Whipples wouldn't have been scared into hiding the stamps and none of this mess would have happened. But then again, none of the good things would have happened, either.

"It hasn't been the vacation I'd planned, that's for sure," she said. She gasped in alarm and squeezed Sam's hand.

"What is it?" Bracing himself, he looked around, expecting to see the Whipples.

"That boy—" Her voice was tense. "Look behind me. See those four boys sitting on a blanket?"

"Sure." Sam realized he was whispering. "I see them, kids just barely into their teens. What about them?"

"The boy on the left, with his hair short on the top and long on the sides." Tara's voice was as tight as a bowstring. "I think he might be the one who swiped my purse. Is he watching us?"

"He doesn't seem to be. Are you sure?"

"No, but it looks something like him. And he's about the same size." Grabbing Sam's hand, she started walking the other way. "Let's get out of here before he sees us. Moss could have told him to keep an eye on us or something."

They hurried around a couple in bathing suits asleep on a blanket and pulled up short when they nearly collided with a youngster running after a beach ball.

Sam cast a glance over his shoulder. The youth Tara had pointed out was still sitting with his friends and there was no sign he'd paid them the slightest bit of attention. No one else on the beach looked suspicious, either. Still, he felt as though he was walking on a high wire. It was almost as if he could feel the Whipples breathing down the back of his neck. But even if the gang was in the hotel this very moment, wouldn't it take Moss a minute to jimmy the door and another minute for them to realize they'd arrived too late?

"You know what I wish?" he said as he and Tara continued rushing along. "I wish I'd thought to tell you to take what you needed from your purse and throw it back where it was. I could have done the same thing with my wallet. That way, the room would have appeared as if we'd never come back."

"You're right." Her legs ached and her shoes kept sinking in the sand. "But it's too late now."

Sam looked over his shoulder again and saw how far they'd come up the beach from the hotel. Anyone looking for them would only see them from a distance. He got an idea.

"Stop a second," he said, bringing Tara to a halt.

She took the opportunity to empty sand from her shoes. When she looked up, she saw that Sam had stripped off his shirt. He looped the sleeves around his waist and stood bare-chested, grinning at her startled expression.

"How's that? Fits in more with the beach crowd, right?"

"It sure does." She wished she had the time to appreciate just how good he looked.

His eyes twinkled. "I suppose I won't have any luck getting you to strip down, too."

"Just once, I ought to shock you."

"It wouldn't be the first time!" He laughed, giving her a quick hug. Then he noticed how her fair hair gleamed in the sunlight. He remembered her trick with the towel. "Do you have a scarf or something?"

She understood at once. Starting to walk again, she opened her purse and pulled out a black-and-tan safari print scarf. She wrapped the scarf around her head and knotted it into a turban.

"That's terrific!" The transformation was even better than he'd hoped. From a distance, it would appear as if her hair were brown and piled stylishly on her head. "And the way you pretended to be a maid was terrific, too."

"Thanks." Their fast pace was keeping her breathless. "The part I liked best was when you played Don Quixote."

"What? Oh, with the mop handle. Maybe it was dumb, but it seemed like a good idea at the time."

"It *was* a good idea. At least you had some sort of defense."

"Yeah, that's what I thought." Still, he was glad that she hadn't seen him attacking the empty bathtub. It had probably looked a little foolish. He supposed there were times when he could get a little carried away.

Tara looked over her shoulder again. Was the boy still back there with his friends? She wished she knew for sure if he was the purse snatcher. Or if he had seen them. Even if he *was* the purse snatcher, it didn't matter if he hadn't seen them. Her thoughts tumbled one after another.

"You okay?" Sam asked, looking down at her, giving her hand a squeeze.

"Yes, I'm okay." She remembered how frightened she'd been when she'd rushed back to his room and found him tied up. Suppose the Whipples had done something awful to him? She realized how dearly she would have regretted the self-control she'd been so proud of in the night. Gasping as she talked, she asked, "Remember how I originally wanted to spend my vacation?"

"To lounge around reading a book?"

"Yes. And letting the world pass me by."

He lifted an eyebrow. "And now you're ready to shout, 'Stop and let me off'?"

"I'm not sure."

"Oh?"

"Well, I can't say this hasn't been . . . different."

He felt his heart give a funny knock against his ribs. She'd given him a swift glance as she'd spoken and for an instant he'd been sure that what she meant was that *he'd* made the difference. A very good kind of difference.

They reached a sprawling hotel terrace where people sat eating. A chef in a tall white hat presided over a smoking grill at the end of a long table.

The aroma of barbecued meat made Tara's mouth water and she said, "What I'm really ready to shout is that I'm starving. We haven't had anything since breakfast. Let's stop long enough to pick up a sandwich." She held up her purse. "My treat."

Sam suggested that they sit while they ate, but once they were seated—side by side facing the beach so they could still keep watch—he got edgy again. Maybe they shouldn't

dawdle, not even for a minute. But they should be safe in the
crowd, shouldn't they? A lot safer than out on the street,
where they would be an easy target. He considered Elmo's
threat about the gun. Was it possible the crook had been
bluffing? He'd never actually revealed the gun, had he?
Damn—if he ever learned it had been a bluff, he would turn
that sneaky weasel inside out.

A sudden whiff of spearmint made the food Sam had just
swallowed sink like a rock in his stomach. He saw Tara's
alarmed expression and knew she'd smelled it, too.

"So there you are!" bellowed a deep voice from behind
them.

They whirled toward the sound, half-jumping from their
chairs. They saw a man in a beach coat wagging his finger
at a little girl who held a green taffy on a stick, her face
sticky with candy. "Daddy's been looking all over for you,"
the man scolded. He scooped her into his arms. "Let's go
back to Mommy," he said. "And I want you to promise us
you won't wander off again."

Sam and Tara stared at each other, their faces still pale
from their scare. "I thought—" they each began in unison,
then they laughed, feeling weak with relief.

"They couldn't have followed us," Sam said. "They
would have had no way of knowing which direction we
went. Still, when I smelled that candy..."

"They could have," Tara said, sobering, starting to get
up. "They could have known which direction we went if the
boy saw us and told them."

"I guess you're right." His eyes searched the beach. "But
that's all they would have had to go on. The boy stayed with
his friends. I kept checking on that. They couldn't have
guessed we'd left the beach and walked up to this particular
hotel." Even though he knew he was right about that, it was

still time to push on. He looked back at Tara. "Do you have
enough money for a taxi to the airport?"

"I'll cash a traveler's check." She was thinking that she
and Sam were at a stalemate and he refused to see it. He
wouldn't listen when she said she wouldn't leave him if he
was going after the Bonbon. The crux of the matter was the
call to Freddy Dwight-Astor. Maybe she could get in on the
conversation. Sam had said that Freddy and his father were
friends. If Mr. Dwight-Astor understood that getting the
ring back meant putting Sam in danger, he would surely
reassess his priorities. Upsetting his wife couldn't compare
with having the son of a friend risk his life. She was certain
he would tell Sam he should go straight to the police.

As they moved quickly up the steps that would take them
inside the hotel, Tara got another thought. Sam had said he
would telephone Mr. Dwight-Astor from the airport, but
why wait? There would be a phone inside the hotel and
they'd be safe for the moment. She would have to think of
some way to get him to call now, before they'd gone any
farther.

It was cool inside the building and Sam slipped back into
his shirt as he accompanied Tara to the front desk. Looking around, he reminded himself that the Whipples couldn't
possibly know where they were now. He found himself
peering suspiciously at a potted palm, as if expecting the ridiculous face of Moss Whipple to pop up among the
branches. He knew he would feel a lot better when they were
away from the beach strip entirely. He would also feel better when he had his own money. The clerk was busy with
someone else and it looked like a wait. Sam told Tara he was
going to the men's room.

"Okay," Tara answered distractedly. She was still trying
to think of a way to persuade him to make the phone call.

"I'll go to the lady's room and freshen up after I get this done. I'll meet you back here in a few minutes."

Few minutes my eye, Sam thought with patient amusement as he walked off, remembering her absolutely necessary half hour in the shower that morning. There was no doubt in his mind that when it came to fixing up, she would be longer than the promised few minutes, even if the hounds of hell were after them.

He looked at his watch. Freddy Dwight-Astor didn't take long champagne lunches—he should be back at his desk. Since he had the time, why wait to call him later? As soon as he left the men's room, he would hunt up a telephone and do it now.

Chapter Nine

Well, things are set," Sam announced, giving Tara a big grin as she joined him at the desk. He linked his arm with hers and they started through the lobby. Things were going great, he thought with satisfaction. He knew what he was going to do and how he was going to do it. All that was left was making sure that he kept Tara out of harm's way.

"I got the clerk to call for a taxi," he said. "There will be one waiting outside."

She gave him a look that he interpreted as worry. It had been a scary afternoon, he thought. Time to lighten things up. His eyes sparkled roguishly. "You know, that dark scarf gives me wild ideas. Have you ever thought of a brunette wig? You could play a maid again. A dark-haired French maid with one of those lacy outfits and garters—"

They'd reached a point far enough from the desk so that Tara felt they could talk. Ignoring his prattle, she stopped and looked him squarely in the eye. "The taxi can wait," she said in a no-nonsense tone. "I know you didn't want to phone until later, but I won't go another step until you've talked with Mr. Dwight-Astor.''

Sam's grin widened. He hadn't intended to explain about the call until they were in the taxi, but what the heck? "Then we can keep right on moving because the call's been made.''

"You—you talked with him already?'' she stammered, taken aback. "But you said you wouldn't do another thing until you'd taken me to the airport.''

A delighted Sam could hardly believe his ears. She was actually in a rush to get to the airport? The afternoon's events must have convinced her that hanging around Miami wasn't such a good idea after all. "That was only because I didn't want the phone call to hold us up,'' he soothed. "Since you were in the rest room, I had the time and everything's set up.''

"What's set up?'' She was so furious with him she could scream. "I wanted to be there when you talked to Mr. Dwight-Astor.''

Sam tilted his head in question. She wanted to be there? What new wrinkle was this?

"You didn't tell him about the gun, did you?'' she accused. "He told you to go ahead and bargain for the ring because you never said a word about the gun.''

Sam's smile faded as he caught her drift. "I don't think there *was* a gun.''

"Of course there was a gun.''

"Did you see it? I sure didn't.'' He set his jaw. "I believed it at the time, but then I started having my doubts. I've read that a lot of professional burglars avoid firearms. It automatically ups the charges if they get caught.''

"They weren't trying to burgle us. They were trying to scare us to death and kidnap us, and of course they had a gun. What's Mr. Dwight-Astor's number? I'm going to call him and give him the full story.''

"I should have known," Sam sighed, looking heavenward. "Look, I didn't have to tell you I'd talked with Freddy. I seriously thought about keeping the call to myself because I was afraid of how you'd react."

"Then why *did* you tell me?"

"Because it's about something important to me and I wanted you to know about it." Standing in a corner of the lobby, he took her hands in his. "Look, I know you believe this is dangerous, but the only real risk is what you said in the first place—that I might lose both the stamps and the ring. If I succeed, I win the entire Dwight-Astor account. Can't you see how much that means to me? I need this break."

"Not this kind of break."

He searched her eyes. "If somebody gave you a chance to be a full owner of that decorating shop right now, you'd jump at it, wouldn't you? All I'm doing is jumping at an opportunity. If Freddy's willing to trade the stamps, I'm willing to take a shot at it."

"What I'm afraid of is that—" Tara's voice choked "—that...that someone's going to take a shot at you!" Her eyes flooded with tears.

Sam felt a soaring sensation somewhere in the region of his heart at this sign of her caring. He pulled her close. "Don't cry. I'll be okay."

Her tears kept coming. "You think you can exchange the stamps for the ring as easy as swapping baseball cards with the kid next door."

"Now, now, no I don't." He patted her back. "I don't think it will be that easy at all. Not at all."

Sniffing, she said, "I bet you don't even have a plan."

"Yes, I do. A good one." He gave her his handkerchief. "Blow your nose. I'll explain it all when we're in the taxi."

She blew her nose. "I'm not paying for a taxi to the airport."

"Okay, forget the airport. I need to go to the bank where Freddy's transferring the money, okay? Just to the bank. And on the way I'll tell you my plan to handle the Whipples."

Tara was filled with dismay as they left the hotel. Sam had convinced himself there would be no problems. There was no gun, the gang could be "handled" like a trio of docile pets and everything would come out exactly right. She didn't want a man who was a coward, but why did he have to be so impossibly fearless?

Outside on the sidewalk she felt even worse. Casting furtive glances, she moved closer to Sam. Where were the Whipples? Maybe they'd already looked in the hotel room and were now out searching the streets. They were criminals, people who shouldn't be messed with. Why couldn't Sam see that? The taxi was waiting and it seemed to her that it took forever before they were safely inside. The cabbie, a sturdy sort with bushy eyebrows, put down the dog-racing sheet he'd been poring over. "Where to, bub?"

Sam gave the bank's address and they started off. Tara was still trying to think of a way to persuade Sam it was too hazardous to deal with the Whipples when she heard him suck in his breath sharply. She looked out the window, seeing they were riding past the Fiesta. Gilbert Whipple was just disappearing under the hotel portico, Moss at his heels.

Gasping, Tara put a hand to her breast, wondering if her heart had stopped. If one of the gang had glanced around at the wrong time they might have been spotted. But it hadn't happened—they were safe. She felt as if a load had slipped from her shoulders. "What a relief!" Her smile suddenly faded. "Were all three of them together? When I think about it, I only saw Gilbert and Moss."

"Elmo was in the lead, going in the door first."

"Are you sure?"

"As sure as I can be."

"They fooled us before."

"Yes, but there's no way they could know where we're going now." Having a plan firmly in mind had given Sam additional confidence.

Tara gave a worried glance out the window, then sagged back in her seat, shaking the scarf from her hair. She looked at the back of the cabbie's thick neck and broad shoulders, glad he was so big, because otherwise, in her state of mind, she would start imagining that *he* could be one of the Whipples. She wondered what he thought of their reactions and conversation. Maybe he'd met his share of oddballs and paid no attention to any of them. She folded the scarf and put it into her purse. "Okay," she said to Sam, "what's this plan of yours all about?"

"I'll have to backtrack a bit," he said, and explained that when he'd left her shop and told Freddy Dwight-Astor he was flying to Miami on the trail of the Bonbon, Freddy had said there was a criminal defense lawyer in Coral Gables who could help if he needed contacts in the Miami area.

Tara made a face. "That was back when you believed I was part of the gang."

Sam chuckled. "But of course, by the time I got here, I'd decided you weren't really a thief."

"Big deal. What you thought was almost worse—thinking I'd let Gilbert Whipple sweet-talk me into transporting he gems."

He laughed at her expression. "It seemed logical at the ime. Anyway, now that I want to confab with the gang, I've old Freddy I'll need his lawyer friend after all. You've probably heard of him—Norman Nelson?"

"Sure. He made a name for himself defending that gang of failed rock musicians who went on a spree robbing convenience stores. He got them off with an astonishingly light jail sentence. But what can he do for us? He may be sharp, but I doubt he's sharp enough to talk the Whipples into giving up the ring."

"That's not what I want," Sam said. "I want him to act as a go-between and set up a meeting between the Whipples and me. The Whipples would trust him because they'd view him as someone sympathetic to criminals."

Tara shook her head. "I think it's too risky to meet them under any circumstances."

"I don't plan to meet them alone, like in some bar. I know better than that. As soon as they learned I know about the stamps, they'd have me out in an alley, knocking the details out of me along with my teeth."

Tara shuddered. "I'm glad you realize you have *some* limitations."

"Some." He grinned. "I'm a lover, not a fighter."

She gave him a look that spoke volumes. "Get on with the plan."

"Nelson can help me work out all the details, but I was thinking he could arrange for us to all meet in his office. I asked Freddy about the value of the stamps. The Dwight-Astor Blues are easily worth double the value of the Bonbon. The Whipples can't help but be interested in a swap."

He interrupted his conversation as the taxi pulled up at the bank. Tara glanced around as they prepared to get out. She couldn't shake the fear that the Whipples would suddenly materialize from nowhere. After she paid the fare, Sam asked the cabbie to wait for them. The cabbie gave them a hard time and they ended up giving him extra money to wait.

"Boy, what a charmer," Tara complained after they were safely inside the bank. She flashed Sam a suspicious look. "And if you wanted that grump to wait because you're still thinking about the airport—"

Sam shook his head. "I said I was giving up on the airport idea, okay? I want the taxi because there's someplace else I have to go after I leave here."

Figuring he meant the lawyer's office, Tara didn't ask further questions as he led her across a floor that looked like black glass and over to a desk where he gave his name and said he wanted to speak with the vice president. Shortly, they were in the bank official's teak-paneled office. The man scrutinized Sam's identification, remarked what a fine fellow Freddy Dwight-Astor was and turned over a cashier's check.

"You know what I don't like about this scheme of yours?" Tara said when they left the office and headed for a teller's line to cash the check. She found herself looking around, automatically checking for the Whipples. "I hate the fact that it doesn't end up with those crooks in jail."

"They'll end up there eventually," Sam answered philosophically. "They'll probably do something to bring it on themselves."

"I still wish we could be the ones to do it. And you know what else? All we've been trying to do is escape them, but now that you want this meeting, how do you let them know? It's not as if you could look them up in the phone book."

Sam bit his lip in consternation. He'd been so busy thinking about what he wanted to say to the lawyer that he hadn't considered how to get his plan off the ground.

"Maybe the car's our answer," he said slowly. "After the Whipples finish scouring the Fiesta, the car will be the only other clue to us that they'll have. They'll eventually have to go back. I can leave them a note on the windshield."

Tara wrinkled her nose, not taking his idea seriously. "Who knows what they'll do? You can't count on them going back. You don't even know that the car will still *be* there."

He looked startled. "What do you mean?"

She shrugged, casting out ideas at random. "For all you know, somebody's stolen it by now. The Whipples are criminals—maybe *they* stole it. Or suppose the gas station attendant reports it abandoned and the city tows it away?"

Sam's face went blank, as if he'd been hit between the eyes. "I never thought about anything happening to the car."

She looked at him oddly. "It certainly seems that the car's the least of our worries."

"Not when the locker key is still under the floor mat."

Tara eyes nearly popped from her head. "But I gave it to you!"

"Shh," he cautioned, seeing they were attracting attention from two blue-haired ladies in line. "I put it back because I figured the key was as safe there as it was with us," he said softly. "When the Whipples showed up, I knew I was right. If they'd caught us again, they would have the key by now."

It was his turn at the window. Turning his back on a still-gaping Tara, he stepped up with the check. When he had his money, he drew Tara over to a quiet corner and started talking fast.

"I'd intended to take the taxi back to the car for the key anyway, and now that you've brought up the idea of something happening to the car, it's doubly important that I get to it fast, which is why I don't want to waste time arguing with you about you staying here at the bank where you'll be safe, because if you refuse to leave Miami, then staying here,

out of the action, is your only option." He ended up winded
because he'd made it all one long sentence.

"Stay out of *what* action?" she demanded, giving another anxious look around.

"I don't know. I hope there won't be any. But we can't
ignore the fact that after hunting around for us at the hotel, the gang would probably return to the gas station. I want
to scout things out without having to worry about you. If I
see the Whipples there, I'll think of something then, but if
things are okay, I'll gas up the car and come straight back
here to pick you up. Then we can hightail it to Norman
Nelson's office and figure out the best way to lay our cards
on the table."

Tara shook her head. She was frightened of the Whipples, but it would be even more nerve-racking waiting
around, wondering what was happening to Sam. "I'm going
with you. I'll be safe if I stay in the taxi."

"Forget it."

"Forget it nothing. If I can't go, there's no point in you
going, either, because you couldn't get in." She played her
trump card. "I've got the car keys, remember?"

He was only momentarily caught off base. "Okay, so you
have them. But you're going to give them to me."

"Oh, and are you going to strong-arm them out of me?
That's what the Whipples would try to do."

They glared at each other. "All right," he conceded, his
tone frustrated. He'd never dreamed of anything like this
when he vowed to teach her to cut loose. He'd created a
monster! "I don't want to waste time fighting over this. But
you stay in the taxi, okay?"

"Okay."

"Fine." His expression was grim. "Now let's get going
and get this over with."

In the taxi his forbidding manner persisted. Tara stared at him, feeling a strange fascination. All of a sudden he'd become a handsome, dark-haired man with an inscrutable expression—her man of mystery. Aware of her attention, he looked over. His attempt to maintain a sour expression failed as a smile teased the corners of his mouth upward. "You're a stubborn lady, you know that?" She had a sudden sense that he would never be able to stay angry at her long. His smile had transformed him back into Sam, and she felt her heart thump.

When they neared the gas station, he said, "If the gang has come back, they're probably in hiding." He told the driver to cruise around the block. With a grunt, the man complied as if the request was all in day's work. Sam decided it would be a good idea for Tara to duck down out of sight, and she cooperated without thinking twice. If the Whipples were around, they would be looking for two passengers rather than one.

Sam saw the yellow sedan parked where they'd left it and he heaved a sigh of relief. The car was safe, no Whipples were in sight and there wasn't a hint of a white car. And to think he'd been so worried. *Hold on, Sam,* he rebuked himself. *Let's not get overconfident.* Who knew what kind of vehicle Gilbert had? And there was no way to tell if anyone was keeping watch from the gift shop. Still, so far so good.

After the taxi took them three-quarters of the way around the block, Sam had the driver park along the side street where there was a view across a corner property to the gas pumps.

"Better keep the engine running," Sam instructed, helping Tara sit up again and thinking that if he saw one of the gang, he would come dashing back for a fast getaway.

"Whatever you say, bub," the man responded matter-of-factly. He picked up his dog-racing sheet.

Sam reached for the door handle and said to Tara, "After I get the car, I'll drive back here for you. Keep your eyes open. If you see anything suspicious, have the driver blow the horn as a warning."

She clutched his sleeve, suddenly feeling terribly afraid for him. "Be careful."

He smiled and briefly caressed her cheek. "Don't worry, I'll be fine." Then he was gone.

Heart in her throat, Tara watched him cut around the back of the station. She realized he was trying to keep out of sight for as long as possible. He disappeared behind a hedgerow of tropical-looking bushes at the far corner, and she knew she wouldn't be able to see him again until he'd gotten the car and moved it to the pumps.

Nervously knotting her sweaty hands, she told herself he would be lost from sight for only a minute—that she'd have to be patient. Trying to calm her fears, she glanced at the cabbie. His arm rested on the back of the seat, revealing a wrist as thick as the leg of a Jacobean table. He hadn't seemed so disagreeable during this part of their trip. He probably wasn't a bad sort when one got to know him better.

Her attention returned to the station. After a moment, the rental car edged into view. Tara raked the area with her eyes, seeing nothing threatening. She watched Sam open the car door and look cautiously around before getting out. The coast must have looked clear because he started putting gas into the car.

Able to breathe once more, Tara impulsively said to the cabbie, "I bet you're wondering what this is all about."

He didn't reply. Attention still on the gas station, she added, "All this cloak and dagger stuff and the engine kept

running, I mean,'' and was immediately annoyed with herself for attempting to continue a conversation that was obviously unwelcome.

The driver surprised her by speaking after all. ''I pay attention to three things, lady,'' he said, not bothering to look
up. ''When people tell me to drive, when people tell me to
stop, and when people try to get off without paying the fare.
All the rest don't mean a diddly-damn.''

Rebuffed, Tara sat stiffly back in her seat. Sam could get
killed out there, and would the cabbie care? Not as long as
he got his money, he wouldn't. She looked back to the station. Her blood ran cold. She'd glanced away for an instant
to talk to the cabbie, and in that brief span of time, Sam had
disappeared. Heart racing, she strained forward. The yellow car was still there, but he was gone. Then she saw him
through the station window. He was inside, paying for the
gas.

Tara sagged back in relief, hand to her throat. Dear God,
if anything had happened to him . . . What would she do
without him? Maybe he wasn't the man she'd always
dreamed of, but he was the one she wanted. She was in love
with him, damn it, and if something bad had happened to
him—

The door on the opposite side of the cab opened. Eyes
widening, she whirled in surprise. Elmo Whipple climbed in.
His hand closed on her arm. ''Surprise!'' he greeted with a
nasty grin. He leaned toward the cabbie, who'd already put
down the racing sheet and was set to go.

''Get moving,'' Elmo ordered.

The taxi started to move ahead.

''Stop!'' Tara cried.

The taxi stopped, throwing Elmo and Tara forward. Tara
twisted her arm free and scrambled out her door. Elmo
started after her.

"Hold it!" ordered the cabbie, collaring Elmo. "Nobody else leaves this car until I get my fare."

Screaming Sam's name, Tara raced toward the gas station. Cutting the corner, she reached the building just as Sam came out, tucking his wallet back into his pants pocket.

"Elmo—he's here!" Half-stumbling, she looked over her shoulder, seeing Elmo finally getting away from the cabbie.

As Sam ran to the driver's side, Tara grabbed for the passenger door. *Locked.* "Open up!" she screamed, tugging the handle. Sam opened the door from the inside and she piled in. They tore off as she slammed the door.

Sam checked the rearview mirror just before he turned the corner. "He's dashing across the street. Maybe his car's behind the gift shop. I don't see the rest of the gang."

Hugging her sides, which ached from her mad dash, Tara was still reliving the moment when Elmo had appeared. "The taxi door just burst open." Trembling, she closed her eyes. "He got in and grabbed my arm. It was like a nightmare."

"It's all right now," Sam said. His eyes were on his driving, but he reached over and patted her hand. "It's okay. We got away and I don't see a car behind us." He frowned. "Maybe I was mistaken when I thought I saw Elmo at the Fiesta. The fellow in front of the others sure looked like him, but maybe it was somebody else. He might have stayed behind here to keep watch." Hands back on the wheel, he turned another corner.

A thought struck Tara and she almost laughed. "Elmo must have had to pay our fare to get away from that cabbie. I was so irritated with that man, but he turned out to be an angel in disguise."

Remembering the locker key, she lifted the floor mat and brought the key out. It was larger than she remembered and the plastic was an even brighter shade of red.

"Now what are you going to do with it?" Sam asked, nervousness making him irritable. "I think it's best hidden away."

"I want it with me." She gave another look around for the Whipples, then rummaged in the bottom of her purse and pulled out a pair of wide rubber bands she remembered getting from somewhere. She looped the bands around her arm, just above her wristwatch, and slipped the key under them. She twisted her arm experimentally. Nothing pinched and the key felt secure. With her sleeve rolled down and buttoned, nothing showed. "There," she said, satisfied.

"I wish this car wasn't yellow," Sam complained. "We're too easy to spot on these residential streets." He checked the rearview mirror as he took another corner. "I'm going to head for a major road, where there's more chance of blending in."

They suddenly heard a funny sound. The car wobbled slightly and slowed.

"A flat tire?"

"It sure sounds like it."

"Have we got a spare?"

Sam steered toward the curb. "I saw one of those damned doughnuts in the trunk. They're only good for emergencies."

Tara stared at him. "This *is* an emergency."

He smiled faintly. "Right." He came to a stop and jumped out to examine the damage. He hopped right back in. "We've been booby-trapped. I didn't give those clowns enough credit. They jammed nails between the treads and one of them pushed through." He started the car moving again.

Tara was confused. "Are we going to try riding with the tire like this? We can't manage highway speeds with a flat."

"I know. I just want to get us off the street as much as possible before I fix it." He pulled into the drive of a house that looked deserted and stopped under the carport. Tall, ragged shrubs that looked like overgrown poinsettias screened them from the street. Their arrival stirred no signs of life and they got out.

Sam tore open the trunk for the jack and the spare, then started working on the damaged tire. Tara shifted nervously, watching the strong movements of his long-fingered hands and the smooth play of the muscles of his shoulders and back. She peeked anxiously through the branches at the quiet street. So far, so good.

When he had the car jacked up and started spinning off the lug nuts, Tara, who'd been around to help change many a tire, rushed to kneel and hold out a hand to put the nuts into the inverted hubcap for safekeeping. He flashed her a quick smile.

"Believe me, I'm not being a chauvinist, but it would help even more if you'd just keep a watch through those bushes for the Whipples."

Shortly, the work was finished. Sam had gotten out his penknife to remove a nail poked in the other front tire, then thought better of it. "As long as it's plugging the hole, maybe it won't go flat so fast. Hell, maybe not at all. We're due a bit of luck."

Tara realized that he hadn't stopped work once to look around. As she moved to get in her side of the car, she said, "My brothers would never have done that."

"Wouldn't have changed a tire?" He threw the jack and old tire into the trunk. "You're pulling my leg. That isn't how you described those guys."

"I mean they would never have trusted me to keep watch. They would have kept looking around, checking for themselves."

"I trust you." He slammed the trunk lid closed. "And I'm not one of your brothers. Let's go."

A few minutes later they came to a busy highway with commercial establishments along both sides. "We're still not far from where we last saw Elmo." Sam's voice was tight with concern. He stopped for the light, then entered the highway and stepped up his speed. As they headed for Coral Gables and the lawyer's office, he started to say something about feeling better when he broke off with a gasp.

"What's wrong?" Tara demanded.

"That white car going the opposite way—it was Elmo, I'm positive."

"Oh, no!" She looked out the back. "Did he see us?"

"In this yellow bomb? How could he miss?" He stomped on the accelerator.

Tara, still looking out the rear window, made a sound of dismay. "He's pulling off the road, trying to turn around."

"There's a curve coming up," Sam said. "Once we get around it, we can zip down a side street and maybe lose him again."

They were around the curve and the echo of Sam's words was still hanging in the air when another sound was heard— the heavy *luff-frump* of another flat tire.

Sam groaned as the car slowed down. Vehicles swerved around them, horns blaring.

Tara pointed at a fast-food restaurant up ahead. "Pull off and park in the back. Elmo won't know where we went."

Ignoring a fiercely blaring horn from a tailgating convertible, Sam pulled off the road and into the drive of the restaurant. The tailgater, also wanting to enter the restau-

rant, zipped around them, not seeing a little foreign car
coming out until too late. There was a screech of brakes and
no collision, but the foreign car stalled and blocked traffic.
The drivers of the two cars began cursing each other. Sam,
unable to get by, opened his window and threw out a curse
of his own.

"This is all your fault in the first place, jerk," the driver
of the convertible yelled, making a rude hand gesture. "Get
that heap off the road."

Both vehicles moved and Sam pulled into the lot and
steered the crippled car around the building.

The area at the rear of the restaurant was considerably
more spacious than the front, with a generous parking area
and a children's playground with brightly colored swings
and slides. Sam parked near picnic tables where family
groups sat eating and watching the children at play. Re-
corded music coming over a loudspeaker mingled with
squeals and laughter.

Sam and Tara left the car and he looked at the ruined tire.
"So much for our run of good luck. This one's even worse
than the other. Even if we knew we were safe, I doubt we
could make it to a station to fix it."

They started across the wide parking lot toward the restaurant's back entrance, where two youngsters sat munch-
ing hamburgers. "I'll feel safer once we're inside the
building," Sam said, veering as a pregnant woman leading
a toddler by the hand crossed their path.

"Maybe we can telephone Norman Nelson," Tara suggested, raising her voice a little to speak over the sound of
the music. "He might send someone to pick us up."

"Hey, terrific idea."

She smiled. "Aren't you glad now you brought me
along—" She broke off as she saw the all-too-familiar white
car coming around the far corner of the restaurant.

Sam saw it, too, and yanked Tara around, ready to run in
the opposite direction. They went a few steps, then stopped
dead. A blue van had just pulled up. Moss and Gilbert
Whipple jumped out.

Sam whirled around again and saw that Elmo had also
left his vehicle. Standing about fifteen feet away, the man
grinned, deliberately flipping open his jacket to reveal the
gun tucked into his waistband.

"I *told* you!" Tara wailed.

Sam looked back at the other two Whipples. They were
closer, only about ten feet away. They had separated and
now simply stood still, moving no closer as they sized up the
situation. Gilbert gave his jacket a brief flip. He had a gun,
as well.

"All these children . . ." Tara moaned.

Sam knew exactly what she meant. All around them were
families with little kids, not one of them paying any attention to the drama happening around them. And not one of
them would be safe if he and Tara put up a fight and one of
the Whipples panicked and bullets started flying.

If only he could attract the kind of attention that would
get people around Tara, protecting her. He thought of the
pregnant woman who had passed by them earlier.

"Quick!" he said to Tara. "Roll down to the ground and
pretend you're in pain. The baby—I'll say the baby's coming early."

"The baby? What—" She stared at him in panicked
confusion, not sure she'd heard him right and not understanding anyway.

His voice rasped in its urgency. "I'll yell that the baby's
coming. People will come running and circle around you.
Let the Whipples capture me. Go on—do it!"

She stared at him helplessly. "But—I can't!"

He turned his head, seeing that Elmo had started moving in. "Come on, you've *got* to!"

It was a crazy idea, yet she could see it might work. But her body seemed paralyzed. Sam took matters into his own hands, throwing his arms about her, one at her waist, one at her back, bending her forward.

"My wife—" he started to yell. "Please, the ba—"

He got no further because Gilbert and Moss had just loomed up on the other side of Tara.

"I have the gun in her ribs," Gilbert warned, his eyes mere slits. "I advise you to back off."

Sam's arms fell as stiffly to his sides as if they were wooden sticks. He stepped away from Tara, seeing her frightened expression. He felt his insides twist with the knowledge of how he'd failed her. All around them, parents and children continued what they'd been doing, nobody giving as much as a passing glance in their direction. The music blared on. Children squealed in play. There was no hope anywhere. In desperation, he looked at Gilbert.

"You don't want her," he pleaded urgently, knowing he had to make the man listen. "I'm the one you want. She gave the key to me and—"

"Shut up," Elmo ordered from behind. Sam felt a gun in his own ribs.

Chapter Ten

Tara held back a sob. They'd been captured and it was all her fault. And it had happened so fast!

Holding them at gunpoint, the Whipples had hustled them into the van. Moss had dumped her in the second row of seats, torn her scarf from her purse and tied her hands in front of her. Then he'd fastened the flowing ends of the fabric around the brace to the front seat headrest. The arrangement forced her to sit forward, her arms elevated, but she guessed it was better than having them tied behind her back. Even better, thank God, Moss had never noticed the key secured to her arm. The rear of the van was open for cargo and that was where they'd put Sam, bound hand and foot.

With Gilbert and Moss in the van, and Elmo following in the white car, they started off. Tara heard Sam groan as he was jolted against the hard metal floor when they went over a speed bump on their way out of the restaurant lot. She tried to turn around and see him, but his body had shifted and she could see only his bent knees.

She bit back another sob. He'd had an idea that might have saved them, but she'd balked and all had been lost. Somebody like Annette would have clutched her stomach and rolled to the ground in an award-winning mock labor scene. But Annette wouldn't have let the Whipples capture Sam, either. That had been the dumb part of his plan. No way should he have thought of getting together with the Whipples on his own.

But it was too late now. She remembered how she'd once decided that she and Sam were mismatched. Well, she thought painfully, she'd been only half-wrong. He'd turned out to be fine for her, but she was bad medicine for him. She just wasn't made of the right stuff.

"You're distracting my driving, Moss," she heard Gilbert complain from the front seat. "Why all the squirming?"

"My gum's lost." Moss patted his pockets and shifted position so he could hunt around in his pants pockets. "There was one stick left and now it's gone."

"So what? You have a wad in your mouth big enough to choke a horse."

"It's not sweet anymore." Moss twisted around again, checking his seat. "I know I had a fresh piece somewhere."

Looking down between her bound arms, Tara inched her shoe over to hide the stick of gum that lay on the floor. She'd seen it fall from Moss's shirt pocket when he'd been rummaging under her seat for the line he'd used to tie Sam. He hadn't noticed and she'd thought nothing of it at the time, but now that he wanted it, she darn well wasn't going to make it easy for him.

"Maybe we could stop someplace," Moss said.

"For chewing gum?" Gilbert laughed rudely.

"I never get what I want." Moss sounded hurt.

"I know something you'll like. There's a battery-operated TV at the hideout."

"Big deal. Elmo won't let me watch the programs I like anyway."

"I'll tell him you should take turns. *Now* what's the trouble? Will you forget about that gum?"

"But I know I had it somewhere." Moss checked the floor under his feet, then started patting his pockets again.

Thinking mean thoughts, Tara wiggled her foot from her shoe. The gum's paper sleeve stuck to the sole of her damp stocking. She dropped the stick inside her shoe and worked her foot back in on top of it. There. It wasn't much of a revenge, but it was something.

Her small victory was forgotten when the van turned onto a side road and stopped in an abandoned housing tract. Appalled, Tara stared out the van window. A single house had been completed and that was in a state of decay, the once-white stucco mildewed a gray green, the jalousie windows mostly boarded over.

Moss got out of the van and came around to unfasten her from the front headrest, but he left her wrists tied. He gestured for her to get out. Trying to hide the fear she felt for both Sam and herself, she climbed down, shuddering as she narrowly missed stepping into a nest of beetles hiding in the weedy grass.

The space once cleared and drained for housing was several acres square and surrounded by brush and tall, skinny thatch palms, their tattered skirts silhouetted against a golden late-afternoon sky. The sinking sun reminded Tara that it was November despite the warm Florida weather. Darkness was all that was needed to complete the *Night of the Living Dead* air to the place. She'd had no idea they would be taken so far from civilization. Was Sam all right?

In the past ten minutes there hadn't been a peep from him, not even when the van had jounced over the rough lane.

Elmo drove up and Gilbert beckoned to him. Tara caught a glimpse of the ruby ring. He wore it on his left hand and she hadn't been able to see it when he'd been driving. After all this trouble she would like to get a good look at it at least once. Gilbert and Elmo hauled Sam from the van. Tara heard him mutter a few choice insults and was cheered by his feistiness.

Gilbert looked over his shoulder. "Bring the girl along, Moss. We'll put them in the back room while we talk things over."

"Okay, but let me show her Princess first."

Elmo snickered and Gilbert smiled. "Why not? We'll meet you inside." Looping their arms through Sam's bound ones, the two crooks dragged him into the ramshackle house.

After Sam was dumped into a room and left, he groaned and started working his body over to the wall so he could sit up and lean against it. His knees and elbows were scraped from being knocked around and his joints ached. He groaned again. The Whipples were aging him fast. What was Moss showing off to Tara? He remembered Elmo's snicker and decided that Princess must be a pit bull. What better mascot for a trio of punks like the Whipples? He looked around. The boarded windows let in only a few cracks of fading light. The furniture was a ladder-back straight chair and scattered packing cases. He heard Tara's voice in the hall and he held his breath, hoping they wouldn't change their minds about putting her in with him.

Moss brought her in. Sam strained his eyes in the dimness. He expected her to be distraught, but she acted as if she'd gained an upper hand.

"Ouch," she said sharply, jerking away from Moss's hold. She'd remembered the gum in her shoe and was feeling a secret satisfaction with every step. "You pinched my arm," she said, accusingly. "I thought nobody was supposed to get hurt."

Moss looked uncomfortable. "I've got to go," he said, backing out the door. He left it open behind him as he retreated down the hall.

"What was that all about?" Sam asked, fascinated.

Tara sniffed the damp, moldering air distastefully. Mindful of the Whipples, whose voices sounded from somewhere down the hall, she said in a low voice, "Let me tell you, if he was all we had to contend with, we'd have the ring and be out of here."

Sam grinned at her tone. Shifting so his bound hands were exposed, he whispered, "You're tied so you can use your fingers. Suppose you explain while you work on these knots. Where did that blockhead take you? Who's Princess?"

"Princess," Tara said with disgust, "is an alligator."

"Jeez. Gators in the canal. I should have guessed."

"It's dozing on the bank not more than fifteen feet from the back of the house. I think Elmo and Gilbert wanted me to see it to scare me, but Moss is actually proud of the horrid thing. He bragged that the crony who lent them this hideout used to toss hunks of meat to lure it into the swimming pool."

"There's a pool in this dump?"

"Used to be. Moss led me in the back way and the pool's falling apart like everything else. Peeling paint, buckling floors, rusty water dripping in a sink of dirty dishes." A new agitation entered her low-pitched words. "This is clothesline you're tied with. The knots aren't going to slip free like the ones in your necktie."

"Do what you can. Maybe getting untied isn't even so smart at this point. There's a better chance of getting them to listen if they think I'm still under their control."

Tara didn't know how much "listening" the Whipples would stand for. "What do you plan to say to them?"

"I'll say I've already turned the stamps over to Norman Nelson for safekeeping. Freddy intended to phone Nelson and tell him about the stamps and the Whipple gang and let him know I'd be in touch. If I can get the Whipples to call Nelson, he'll be clever enough to play along and agree he has the stamps."

He stopped talking as footsteps came down the hallway. A circle of light entered first, then the three Whipples, Moss carrying a kerosene lamp. In the flickering light, the smiles on the faces of the crooks were as sincere as the grins cut into Halloween jack-o'-lanterns.

"About time," Sam said, his unexpectedly firm tone taking them by surprise. "I've got some things to say to you characters."

"Do tell," Gilbert said. He turned the chair around and sat straddling it. "So you're Sam Miller." He peered down at Sam with scorn. "We have things to say to you, as well. For example, are you ready to surrender the stamps? And don't claim you don't have them. Elmo related the routine the girl went through with her notebook." He gave Tara a look that sent her cowering against Sam. Moss was one thing, Gilbert quite another. "The two of you found the Blues and hid them, that's obvious. The question is, where?"

Sam's eyes had turned hard. The rumors were true—Gilbert imagined himself some sort of gentleman. Sam could play that game, too. "You need only ask. We turned them over to a partner, the renowned lawyer, Norman Nelson. Does the name ring a bell?"

Gilbert frowned. "How are you associated with him?"

"He's the man I needed for a deal like this." Would it help if he presented himself as a fellow crook? He cleared his throat. "It's fine with me if you end up with the stamps. But in order to turn them over, there's a bit of business that comes first." Up until this point, he had kept his gaze from the ring, but now he allowed his eyes to fasten on it. "I have a . . . client who's fond of rubies. I thought we could make a trade."

"The Blues for this?" Gilbert thoughtfully studied the ring on his hand.

"Exactly." Feeling increasingly confident about how things were going, Sam referred to the comparative value of the two items, then shut his mouth. He figured all that was needed now was for Gilbert to call Norman Nelson, and the job was nearly cinched.

"Tell you what," Gilbert said after a long silence. "I have a client, too—one who's fond of stamps. But then again, I'm fond of this ring. I don't want to trade unless it's absolutely necessary."

Sam made the best shrug he could manage with his arms tied. "Sorry, but it's out of my hands. Nelson's holding the stamps for the deal I described."

"Interesting." Gilbert stood. "There are people I must see this evening. Since you two brought me down to Miami, I'm meeting with local talent to discuss future possibilities. I'll check your story out with Norman Nelson and return by morning."

"Morning?" Sam was dismayed. "If we're going to make a deal, you can't expect—"

"Please, please, Mr. Miller. I said I'd check out your story, didn't I? Moss, we can't leave the girl like that. Tie her to something."

"Okay, boss." Setting down the lamp, Moss took the chair Gilbert had vacated and turned its back to Tara, who still sat on the floor. He pulled her bound hands up and firmly knotted the ends of the scarf to one of the ladder-back rails, placing the knots so she couldn't reach them with her teeth.

Nodding in approval, Gilbert gave Tara a menacing grin. "If any ideas about a midnight stroll come to you, you'll have a built-in walking partner with four wooden legs."

"That's rich," Elmo chortled as the trio left the room, taking the lamp with them.

With the scent of kerosene gone, the moldering odor of the room returned, stronger than ever in the darkness. Tara remembered the hungry way Sam had looked at the Bon-bon. It was the prize that guaranteed so many good things in his future. If he lost it, it would be because of her.

"Believe me," Sam said wryly in the hushed darkness, "this isn't exactly what I had in mind."

"It's not your fault," she said, fighting back tears of helplessness. Her arms were strained from being held up to the back of the chair. She tilted the chair over so that it and her bound hands rested in her lap. "I should have done what you wanted at the restaurant."

"Why wouldn't you?" He sounded sincerely puzzled. "You pretended to be a maid at the hotel and that wasn't nearly so important."

"That was different," she said softly. "It wasn't in public. But I should have gone ahead and done it anyway."

"Well," he said after a thoughtful silence, "maybe it wouldn't have worked. The Whipples still could have whisked us into their van before anyone came to the rescue."

That's what Tara thought, too, but she was relieved to hear Sam confirm it. Footsteps left the house and they heard the sound of a car engine. "Gilbert must be leaving," Tara said. "Maybe Moss and Elmo will go out, too, to get food."

"Bet they won't bring back anything to share."

"Bet they won't, either. I'd like to have something to drink, but maybe that's just as well because—" She broke off.

Sam finished the sentence. "Because you bet they won't take us to the bathroom."

"That *is* what I was thinking," she admitted. "They wouldn't go to the trouble to untie me, and with this chair—" She broke off again.

Sam chuckled. "You'd need a lot of help."

"I sure would." She couldn't help giggling. "I can't believe I'm finding something funny in this situation. I thought you were too much like my brothers, but you're not. Not really." It seemed like a tremendous confession to her, but he took it in stride, having no idea what it meant.

"You make them sound like great guys," he said. "You've got this sister thing, poking at them a little, but there's a soft look in your eyes when you talk about them, even when you're telling something about them that annoys you."

She hadn't expected his perception. "I love them a lot, but they're always cutting up and clowning around and—well, they can be crude."

"I've guess I've got my crude moments, but you don't bring it out. You know what one of the first things that I thought about you was? Besides thinking how beautiful you are, that is. You made me think of pearls, white gloves and champagne."

She didn't respond. She knew he meant his words as a compliment, but what they added up to was that she was too formal for him, too reserved.

He said, "Do you think you can work that chair around so you could still reach my ropes?"

"Maybe, but it won't get us anywhere. There isn't enough free movement for my fingers to work together. And the rail keeps my hands at too much of an angle."

"I've got a penknife in my pocket. If you can manage to work it out and get it open one-handed, maybe you can saw through the rope."

Tara felt a surge of hope at his plan and had just moved over to him when they heard footsteps and saw a flashlight moving down the hallway. They sprang apart. Moss walked in, carrying a television set and a folding chair. He shone the flashlight into their faces. "Don't you think *The Munsters* is a good show?"

Sam squinted against the light. "It has its moments."

Moss beamed. "That's what I think, too. But Elmo only makes fun."

Moss switched on the TV, opened the folding chair and sat down. Tara and Sam exchanged long-suffering glances. The antics of the spooky Munster family had just started when Elmo, carrying the lantern, came in.

"I thought we were going to the store."

"After I watch this."

"You've seen that a million times."

Moss folded his arms stubbornly, the eerie light of the television flickering over his face. "That's how I know I like it."

"Come on," wheedled Elmo. "Quit wasting batteries on a rerun. Take the TV into the kitchen. We'll watch quiz shows together when we come back."

Moss hesitated. "No laughing at the answers I call out?"

"I promise." While Moss carried the TV and his other things out, Elmo checked to make sure Sam and Tara were still tied, then left, too. Shortly, the house door slammed and the van drove away.

"They won't be gone long if they're coming back for the quiz shows," Sam said. "Hurry and see if you can get my penknife."

The urgency in his voice told Tara he wasn't as confident of his scheme with Norman Nelson as he pretended. She hadn't realized until then just how much she'd been depending on his optimism. Trying to keep her voice steady, she quipped, "What is this—hedging our bets?"

"Hell, no," he said with a chuckle, his tone so deliberately light that she knew he'd detected her fear. "I'm all set for my morning talk with that stuffed shirt, Gilbert. I just hate spending the night with a woman when I'm too tied up to hug her."

"Okay." She found she could smile once again. "Let's give it a try."

It wasn't any easier than she'd thought it would be, but with both her and the chair on their sides, and Sam on his back with his legs thrown over the chair seat, she was able to reach her fingers into his side pocket, where he kept the penknife.

"Hmm," he said, "this has possibilities." He angled his hips, lifting slightly to give her better access. "Your fingers are warmer than I'd expected."

Ignoring him, Tara said, "I can feel it through the cloth, but I can't reach far enough inside. Jounce a little and maybe it will slide into my hand."

"Oh, talk to me, baby, talk dir—"

"Will you shut up," she said with a giggle, cutting off his words. "Who said I didn't bring out the crudeness in you? If you keep making me laugh, I can't do what I'm trying to do."

"You feed me those terrific leading lines and I'm supposed to ignore them?"

"Yes. Now, don't move." She just barely touched the end of the penknife with her extended fingertips. "This is serious business here." She closed her fingertips scissors-fashion around the penknife and drew it backward, flexing her hand. It took several attempts, but the knife finally dropped to the floor.

"Can you get it?" Sam asked, no longer kidding around.

"No, but you can. It must be right under you. Lift your legs and I'll move the chair. You're tied so your fingers can move together. Find the knife and open it, then give it back to me."

He handed the knife up to her and she started sawing on the rope. She could use only the tip of the blade because of the limitations of the chair rail. In the darkness, she couldn't tell if she was sawing in the same place or not. She'd only just gotten started when the Whipples returned.

Elmo, holding the lantern, came in to check on them. Sam and Tara had sprung apart, Sam palming the knife and pretending to be sleeping. Elmo gave only a cursory glance at their bonds, then left, once again leaving the door to the dark hallway open. The noise of the TV blared. They heard Moss calling out responses to the program.

"No invitations to share dinner," Sam said with a disgruntled sigh as he moved over to Tara again and passed her the knife.

"They probably didn't even think of us," she said. "Just food for the two of them."

"And Princess. If this were a movie, I could rub a cut finger on the ropes and old Princess would lumber in and make short work of my bonds."

"And short work of you." Tara giggled. "I just thought of what else they probably bought at the store—gum for

Moss." She told Sam about the stick of gum she'd hidden
in her shoe.

"That's beautiful!" He tried to hold back his laughter.
"Oh, my Lord, that's absolutely beautiful." Tara was
laughing, too, the tension and the danger seeming to recede
for the moment. "The more I imagine him scrambling
around, trying to find his precious gum, while all the
while—" He broke off as Moss, flashlight in hand, came
down the hallway. Tara and Sam waited in terror, sure their
plan to get free had somehow been guessed.

Moss came in and flashed his light in their faces. "The
saying goes, 'A snitch in time,' right?"

Sam, blinking against the glare, remembered that the
crooks had been watching a quiz show. "You mean the
saying, 'A *stitch* in time?'"

"No, no!" Moss stamped his foot. "A *snitch*, not *stitch*.
Who cares about sewing stuff? But if a snitch tells you
something in time, especially a warning about the cops, it
can make a real difference, right?"

"I see what you mean." Sam tried not to laugh. "Maybe
the guy who thought of the answer on the program wasn't
a man of the world like you."

Moss beamed. "Boy, that's the truth. I'll explain it that
way to Elmo."

Tara and Sam had just gotten back together when they
heard Moss returning.

"I can't believe this," Tara wailed, gritting her teeth as
they jumped apart again.

Moss trundled in, bringing along the TV. An old John
Wayne cowboy film had come on. Elmo wanted to go to bed
and Moss didn't want to watch the movie alone.

By the time the movie was over, a thoroughly disgusted
Tara and Sam were pretending to be asleep and very nearly
were. Moss dragged off the TV, flashlight and folding chair.

When all was quiet in the house again, the two prisoners moved back together. Sam, sitting with his back to Tara, waited for her to start sawing his ropes.

"Okay," he said impatiently.

She stretched her fingers down toward his hands, ready to grasp the knife. He didn't extend it up to her promptly as he'd done the last time.

"I'm ready," she said, as impatient as he. She felt his body tense.

"You don't have it?" he asked.

"No. When Moss came in the last time, I dropped it down to your hands like before. I thought—" She muffled a cry. "That idiot crook, messing us up. The knife could be any-where!"

"Calm down. Not anywhere. It's either under us or somewhere between here and where we moved when we heard him coming."

His logic was perfect, but in the darkness they had no success. They finally gave up the search in a state of ex-haustion.

"We'll have to wait for daylight," Sam said. He sat propped against the wall, Tara's head pillowed on his shoulder.

"Does it hurt you, my leaning this way?" she asked.

"No, I'm fine. This is perfect." He rested his cheek against her hair. She could feel his breath as he talked. "Everything's going to be all right," he said. "You'll see."

She could only hope he was right.

When the first slender light filtered through the cracks of the boarded windows, Sam painfully opened his eyes. The wooden floor under his head felt as hard as a brick. Chilled and aching, he suppressed a groan. For a moment, he couldn't remember where he was or why he was there. Every bone and muscle in his body cried out in resentment. The only place where he felt warm was his back. It was Tara, he realized—Tara pressing against him, probably every bit as cold and aching as he.

Everything came back to him then—where they were and why. "Tara," he whispered urgently. "Tara, wake up."

She murmured in drowsy complaint. The legs of the chair scraped as she moved. All at once, she was totally awake.

"The penknife," she said urgently.

"We'll find it," he said, struggling to sit up. "It must be pretty early yet, but it's light enough to see."

Still trying to work the life back into their stiff bodies, they looked around the room. Sam spotted the blade, caught in a slot where the baseboard and warped floor had separated.

"No wonder we couldn't find it in the dark," he said with annoyance, shoving himself backward to the spot where the knife lay. His fingers were stiff, but he located the knife by touch and pried it from its hiding place. "It must still be pretty early. What time is it?"

Tara looked at her watch and cried out in dismay. "It's not early at all, Sam! It's nearly seven o'clock."

Sam cursed, realizing he hadn't considered that only a small amount of early light would creep in through the cracks in the boarded windows. He moved to Tara and handed the knife up to her.

Working with a sense of quiet desperation, Tara ignored the strain in her cramped fingers as she sawed on a strand of rope that bore ragged signs of her blind starts and stops during the night. Ironically, now that she could see what she was doing, her fingers were so much stiffer that she still couldn't do a good job. Escape was their only hope, she thought. Sam must finally be admitting to himself that the

Whipples would never play fair and that getting away was their only real option.

"Stop working on the rope now," he said quietly.

"It's almost worn through," she objected, sure she hadn't understood him.

"Good, but I want you to use the time to get the locker key and give it to me. I've thought things over—I'm making you part of the deal now. I want you turned loose and out of here before I agree to go to the lawyers."

It was a foolish notion, she thought, one that would lead to a dead end. She shuddered at the thought. Besides, she wasn't leaving him under any circumstances.

"The strands are finally parting," she said. "Just a minute more."

"I can feel the slack. You've done enough." He shifted so she could no longer reach his bonds. "It's the key I want now." He turned to face her.

She stared at him, seeing his handsome face leaner and rougher in the early light, the stubble of his unshaven beard dark along his jaw.

"As long as you have the key, you're involved and you stay involved. I want the key in my possession. I won't do a thing more with the Whipples until I see you go safely out that door."

There were times when his ideas were good, but this one was so impractical that she wanted to tear her hair. "Then let me finish cutting you loose," she hissed. "Then you untie me and we *both* leave!"

"Do you think we'd stand a chance of getting out?" His chuckle held a raw edge that made her shiver. She realized he would never walk away from the ring, not after coming so far.

"Now give me the key," he ordered. The set of his jaw and the look in his eye convinced her there was no point in further argument. Whatever was to happen, it was best that she get his bonds loose, and until he had the key, he wouldn't permit that to happen.

Sitting with the back of the chair resting in her lap, she set to the task. Unable to unfasten her sleeve, she had to work through the fabric, pulling the locker key free from the rubber bands with her teeth. The key had slipped loose and she was working it down from the inside of her sleeve when a car pulled up outside.

"Hurry!" Sam urged.

She was too busy to reply. The key poked through the sleeve opening and dropped to the floor. She slid the chair out of the way. "It's behind you. To your left."

The house door slammed and Gilbert's voice could be heard. Sam looked over his shoulder and saw the key. He edged backward. His fingers closed on the key and he drew it into his hand.

Muted grumbles and mumbles came from another part of the house as Gilbert woke up the other two.

"Your ropes," Tara pleaded. "The last strand is ready to give. Give me a chance and I'll have it cut through."

"If it parts all the way, they may see it. It's too much of a risk. I have to look as if I'm playing along. Kick the knife over against the baseboard and toe it into that crack again."

By the time Gilbert and Moss entered the room, Sam, curled against the wall, appeared as calm and collected as a man can be when he's tied hand and foot. Tara, white-faced and stoic, stared unblinkingly at her bound hands. She remembered the edge to Sam's chuckle. The deal for the ring meant so much to him. She prayed his plan would work and the ring would be his. And failing that, she prayed that they wouldn't end up being left as food for Princess.

"Good morning, Mr. Miller," Gilbert greeted him, his one condescending. "I trust your accommodations have been satisfactory?"

"I've had better."

"That well may be." Since the room's only chair was in use, Gilbert signaled to Moss, who promptly pushed over one of the packing cases for him to use as a seat.

Sam raised a brow. "Where's Elmo?"

"On an errand. Nothing to do with you, Mr. Miller. You're not the only matter of interest to me in the Sunshine State." Gilbert crossed his legs and cupped a knee, the bonbon on deliberate display, the deep red of the ruby a sullen fire in the poorly lit room. "You may recall your suggestion that I make a call to a certain lawyer?"

Sam narrowed his eyes. "I remember. And now I've got something to add to the deal."

"Oh? Something to my advantage or yours?"

Sam was sick of Gilbert's fancy act. "Something to your advantage, creep. That is, if you still want the stamps."

"Show some respect for the boss," Moss scolded indignantly, kicking Sam's leg. Sam moved quickly enough to lessen the blow, but it still sent a wincing pain along the already cramped muscle. Boy, he thought acidly, Moss would have a good long wait before Sam would ever be *his* TV buddy again.

"Now, now," Gilbert chided. "We're attempting to have a pleasant discussion, aren't we, Mr. Miller? Do you think we can continue without the name-calling?"

"Yeah, right," Sam said, then wary of Moss, added quickly, "Okay, no names."

"Fine. Now, I still want the stamps, of course, but first there's something you should know. I've already phoned Norman Nelson." Gilbert's smile was repulsively self-satisfied as he dropped his bombshell. "I introduced my-

self as Sam Miller. He said he'd been waiting for my call. He
also said he hoped I'd had the sense to put the stamps
somewhere for safekeeping. I assured him that I had and
hung up.''

Sam felt as if he'd been socked in the stomach. The game
was ended. Or was it? He forced a grin. ''Sounds like we've
cut out the middleman. Now you deal directly with me. The
stamps are yours for two things—the ring and letting Tara
go.''

Gilbert cocked his head. ''I remember you trying to say
yesterday that we didn't want the girl, we wanted you. Such
chivalry.'' He frowned. ''You also mentioned a key?''

Sam felt in control again. ''The stamps are in a public
locker. When I see Tara walk out of this room with your car
keys in her hand—when I hear her start up the car and
leave—that's when I tell you where the locker is.''

''He's bluffing,'' Moss said. ''I can tell.''

''Moss has a point, Mr. Miller. Once we let the girl go,
we'd have nothing except your promise. You'll have to do
better than that.''

Sam weighed his options. Why not turn over the key?
They still wouldn't know where the locker was. They would
have fun running to lockers at dog tracks, jungle gardens,
bus stations, exhibition centers.... There were public at-
tractions all over Miami.

''Cut her hands free to prove your good faith,'' Sam said.
''Then I'll give you something tangible.''

After a moment's thought, Gilbert took a switchblade
from his pocket and tossed it to Moss. Tara could hardly
believe what was happening when her bonds were cut.
Trembling, she pushed the chair aside and stumbled to her
feet. Moss's hand closed tightly on her arm.

''There's my good faith gesture,'' Gilbert said.

Sam fought back an order that Moss take his filthy hands from Tara's arm, but getting himself kicked around further would help neither of them. "Okay, I'll give you the key. But you won't know where the locker is unless I tell you." Inspiration came to him. "Furthermore, by now, Norman Nelson has probably decided my phone call sounded funny. He'll check it out with my client, who *does* know where the locker is. If you don't accept my deal fast, you'll get to the locker and find somebody waiting who's a lot bigger than you."

"Oh?" Gilbert became rigid, clearly unhappy with the thought of someone else reaching the locker first. "And what of the ring?"

"The hell with the ring!" Sam felt a red rage of frustration rise in him. "Just let her go. Can't you see I wouldn't fool around with her safety? Forget the ring—just set her free!"

Tara's smothered gasp was lost in the tension in the room. Sam was willing to give up the ring for her?

"Ah, young love." Gilbert stood. "Very well, where's the locker key?"

Sam looked up from his position on the floor. "Hand her your car keys. Let her walk out the door."

"I must be assured you have this locker key first, Mr. Miller."

Sam hesitated, then moved aside. The key lay on the floor, where he'd apparently been sitting on it all the while.

Gilbert studied the key thoughtfully. "And how did it come to be there?"

"It fell from my shirt pocket in the night."

Tara realized that Sam was deflecting attention away from his hands, trying to keep Gilbert from seeing that the rope had been tampered with.

Eyes shifting between the two of them, Gilbert smiled as he stroked his jaw. Tara had a fleeting impression that he was playing with them, but then the possibility of freedom overwhelmed all else. She had been wrong when she'd thought earlier that she couldn't leave Sam. Now she saw it was her one chance to save him.

Gilbert pulled the car keys from his pocket and tossed them to Moss, who handed them to her. "On your way," Gilbert said with a leer. "Quick, before I change my mind."

Tara cast a look toward Sam, trying to convey all the love she felt for him along with the silent promise that she would soon have help speeding on its way. Then she was rushing down the echoing hallway, through the living room and across the entry, flinging open the front door, ready to flee the filthy, ramshackle house, rushing toward safety for both Sam and herself.

She stepped on the porch.

"Oh, no!" She gasped in horror, bringing herself up short. "Oh, no—"

Chapter Eleven

Well, Mr. Miller?'' Gilbert asked impatiently.

Expression intent, Sam shook his head, busy listening. He'd heard Tara run through the house. Then he'd heard the front door open and close. Something was wrong, yet he couldn't quite put his finger on it. Was she taking too long to get the car started? No, she'd been shaky when she'd left the room and her fingers and wrists had to be stiff from being bound—she was probably having trouble turning the ignition. So why did he keep thinking there was something that he'd missed?

He heard the engine start, then the sound of the car pulling away.

"The location of the locker, Mr. Miller?"

Glaring, Sam stalled a bit longer. He could no longer hear the car. Tara must be in the clear. He returned his attention to Gilbert. He remembered telling Tara that none of the Whipples had a record of harming anyone, but he imagined Gilbert had had his share of unrecorded moments.

With Tara safe, Sam figured he'd better start thinking of his own skin.

"A deal's a deal. The stamps are in a locker at Miami International."

"Indeed. And how did they come to be there?"

Sam edited the truth to match his shady guise as a fellow criminal. "Tara discovered the stamps as we were flying down here. I recognized them as the stolen Blues. We stashed them in the airport locker and were trying to find a buyer when you showed up with the ring. We didn't have the best contacts for selling stamps, but I did have a market for the ruby. A trade seemed like a bright idea."

"Perhaps not so bright after all." Gilbert looked down at the locker number printed on the key, then looked up again, his smile becoming increasingly despicable. "It seems as if our business is finished, Mr. Miller."

The word "finished" had such a final sound, Sam thought, wishing he could get over the nagging sense that he'd overlooked a significant detail.

"Very well, Moss," he heard Gilbert say. "Call Elmo back."

That's when Sam recognized his error. How could he have been so stupid? He knew damned well that the comings and goings of every vehicle could be heard. If Gilbert had actually sent Elmo off on an errand, they would have heard him leave. That was what he'd missed, the sound of Elmo driving away. Gilbert had anticipated his demand for Tara's freedom and had kept Elmo outside, lying in wait.

Gut twisting, Sam heard Moss open the front door. He imagined the man signaling to the car waiting somewhere down the road. Sure enough, the sounds of the returning vehicle followed almost immediately. Sick at heart, Sam closed his eyes. Tara had never stood a chance.

A grinning Elmo escorted Tara into the room. A rag was fastened across her mouth and her hands were tied again, this time behind her back. Her eyes had a dazed look, as if she'd been struck. Elmo pushed her to the floor. The rage Sam had experienced earlier returned thousandfold.

"She doesn't look in the mood to skip off at the moment, but tie her feet anyway," Gilbert said. Elmo lashed her ankles together with lengths of torn sheeting. She lay limply, offering no resistance. Sam's pulse thundered dangerously. He would get even with them somehow, by God, he would.

"That's that," Gilbert said with satisfaction when Elmo was finished. He brushed his hands as if he were the one who had done the work.

A new concern gripped Sam. He couldn't let Gilbert guess he wasn't as helpless as he appeared. Swallowing his fury, he feigned panic. "You're not going to leave us here, are you? You can't do that!"

"Sniveling, Mr. Miller?" Gilbert looked pleased.

"Give us a break, Whipple. This place is in the middle of nowhere. Nobody knows we're here. We don't even have water!"

Gilbert shrugged. "The house isn't locked. Perhaps you'll be able to work yourselves down to the canal."

"And Princess," Elmo said with a snicker.

Gilbert smiled. "I'll tell you what, Mr. Miller. Considering your unsavory interest in both the stamps and the ring, you'll probably have no inclination to cause us trouble. If we find the Blues where you've said they are, we just might—*might*, I say—alert a friend to come and rescue you." He glanced at his watch. "Remembering what you've said about Norman Nelson getting suspicious, we'd best be on our way."

The three crooks left and it seemed the longest wait in Sam's life before he heard the car drive off. Then he was all action.

"I'll have my ropes undone in a second, Tara, honey," he promised, straining against the bonds she'd loosened so effectively that morning. He was relieved to see the glazed expression fading from her eyes. Feebly, she struggled to sit up.

"It's okay, stay relaxed," he soothed. "I'll be with you in a flash." She made a strangled sound of assent.

Despite the slack, Sam had more trouble with the rope that he'd expected, then something slipped. He worked one hand free and flung the tangled rope aside. Retrieving his penknife, he made short work of the knots around his legs. Then he was beside Tara, cutting her bonds, taking the gag from her mouth.

"Sam—" she croaked in a half sob, burrowing into his arms.

"It's okay," he soothed, closing his eyes, thinking how wonderful it was to hold her. "What did Elmo do to you? Did he hit you?"

"He just knocked me down. But I was scared—Sam, I was so scared!" Her words were half-muffled against his chest. "I wanted to escape so badly, to get help back to you." She lifted her head. "I ran out the door and nearly stepped on that vile alligator! It was lying next to the steps, gnawing on food tied to the porch post. Moss's idea of a guard dog." She shuddered. "But I still believed I was free until I saw the van next to the white car. Then Elmo was there, knocking me down, gagging me before I could scream." Tears clouded her eyes. "The least I could have done was scream so you'd have known not to give Gilbert any more information."

"It's okay, honey." He hugged her hard. "If I hadn't talked, Gilbert would have tried socking it out of me anyway. The important thing was to get rid of them so I could get loose." He got to his feet, helping her up, as well. He stretched his cramped muscles and started rubbing his wrists and ankles. His expression was thoughtful. "I only heard the car drive off. They must have left the van."

Tara gave him a swift, hopeful glance. "We're taking the van and finally going to the police, aren't we?"

He took her hands, gently smoothing the reddened patches where the scarf had chafed her skin. He looked into her eyes. "If we go to the police now, everything that's happened now will be for nothing. You can see that, can't you?"

"You're still thinking of meeting with them after all this?" She hugged herself as if she were cold.

"I'm not meeting with them. All I'll be doing is following them to the airport. I've got nothing to lose, and what can happen in so public an area? Maybe I'll get some brilliant last-minute idea. If I don't, then we call the police. If you hate the idea so much, I can drop you off at a safe place, if you want."

She glared at him. "Sam Miller, you know darned well that no matter what you do, I'm going with you."

He grinned. "Okay. What are we waiting for?"

On their way out she stopped in the bathroom and when she came outside, Sam was crouched inside the van, messing with the steering column. She opened the side of the van to get her purse from where Moss had tossed it. "Can you hot-wire it and get it started?" she asked.

"I had to pull the ignition. For once I'm glad these guys are thieves—they had the kind of tools in the back that I needed." He wiped his hands and got up into the seat. "How'd you know about hot-wiring?"

Purse in hand, she took her place beside him. "Buddy once had an old car with a bum ignition. Fiddling with the wires was the only way he could make it run." She eyed Sam curiously. "How'd you know how to, um, pull the ignition?"

He flashed her a quick look and a grin. "Think I was born an insurance man?" He turned a screwdriver in the ignition cavity and the engine roared to life. They started off.

"Take a right here," she said at the end of the decrepit lane, remembering the route the van had followed the day before. She reached into her purse for a comb, sending Sam a sideways glance. Even unshaved and with clothing the worse for wear, she found him appealing. She remembered the first impression she'd had of him, when she'd taken him for a picture-perfect dream man. After all those years with her wacky crew of siblings, her plastic fantasy hero would have bored her to extinction after five minutes.

Within a quarter mile they were back in civilization, the scrubby ruin of the housing development lost behind the trees. Tara shuddered, thinking she never wanted a reminder of the horrid place. Bending down, she removed Moss's stick of chewing gum from her shoe and stuffed it into the ashtray. It had given her satisfaction for a time, she thought, wrinkling her nose, but now it was simply another reminder.

She glanced up at the road again. "Take another right up here, then you'll probably know where you are."

Sam, his attention on his driving, acknowledged her direction with little more than a grunt. She sent him a swift look, seeing that his face had once again taken on that hard, uncompromising aspect that was both a warning and a fascination.

She revised her earlier thoughts, reminding herself there was a lot more to him than good looks and laughter. There was tenderness as well as the toughness she was seeing now. And when it came to the way he'd made her feel when he'd been willing to abandon the ring for her sake...she couldn't begin to put those wonderful feelings into words.

They entered the highway and he stepped hard on the gas. They'd gone about a third of the distance to the airport when they ran into an early-morning traffic jam.

"Somebody's probably had a breakdown," Tara speculated nervously. "Of all times."

"It may work *for* us if the Whipples are caught in it, too. usually hate people doing what I'm about to do now, but—" He pulled off the road onto the shoulder and started to ride along the outside, passing other cars. Reaching a side street, he turned off. "Let's hope the Whipples are caught someplace in the middle of that mess."

After driving a distance, he was able to cut over to another highway that would approach the airport by a different route.

His manner had relaxed and Tara realized that the traffic jam had given him the hope that the Whipples' head start had been erased. After a few more miles, she ventured, "That business about Norman Nelson getting suspicious and somebody watching the locker—was that all a bluff?"

He shrugged. "Anything's possible, but I was mostly putting pressure on Gilbert."

After a few more minutes of hard driving, they started seeing airport signs. Sam slowed. The airport turn came up. Sam flipped his turn signals. Tara wondered what he was thinking. If the authorities were waiting for the Whipples, the ring would become part of official evidence. Mrs. Dwight-Astor would learn it had been stolen and Sam's goal of winning the Dwight-Astor business would evaporate like a cloud.

As they approached the terminal, Sam said abruptly, "There are a few things I need. You have stationery in your notebook, don't you? I need an envelope. And quarters. I've got bills, but no change."

Puzzled, she rummaged in her purse. She was about to question his purpose, but then he said, "Write your name and address on the envelope and put a stamp on it." She found a pen and did as he requested and was passing it over to him, ready to ask what was going on, when she saw they neared the section of the airport where she'd hidden the Blues.

"This is where I came out after I left the locker," she said, peering out her side window, nerves starting to twang. She gasped. "That white car in the no-parking zone—it's the Whipples!"

"We didn't beat them after all," Sam said, stomping on the brake. "The car's empty—they must already be inside."

Spinning the wheels, he bumped the van up on a concrete island. The chauffeur of a stretch limousine steered around them and tooted an angry horn.

"At least we're not in no-parking," Sam said, not taking time to turn off the engine as he grabbed for the van door. "Come on," he called to Tara as he vaulted to the ground. But she was already out her own door and in the street, stretching her arms out to stop an oncoming car, making a clear path by the time Sam dashed around. The heck with restraint in public.

Sam grabbed her hand and they slipped past the stopped car's bumper as they dashed across the street. The day she'd been there before, that part of the airport had been nearly

deserted, but now the sidewalk was clogged with passengers and baggage.

Breaking hands with Sam, Tara scuttled through a cluster of teenagers. A white Persian cat in a wire carrier cow-
ered and squalled, losing at least three of her nine lives as
Sam thundered upon her and leaped over her enclosure.

Inside the terminal, it was just as congested. "The lockers are right ahead," Tara said, grabbing his shirt. "If you
don't want them to see us—"

Sam grabbed the wall to slow himself. Screeching to a
halt, he stood on tiptoe, scanning over the heads of the
crowd. He saw them—all three of the Whipples. They
headed toward the wall of lockers, marching as neatly as
ducks in a shooting gallery.

Sam turned to Tara. "Keep out of the way. Things may
get rough." Then he was leaving her behind, swiftly working his way through the crowd. He ducked under the arm of
a man reading a paper. Still keeping low, he came up in front
of the lockers about eight feet down from where he'd seen
the Whipples heading. An unused locker, the key in the
door, was before him. Reaching up, he slipped in his quarters.

He ducked back and managed to see the Whipples coming up to the lockers. Then a man with a garment bag over
his shoulder got in between him and the crooks. He couldn't
afford to wait for a clear view—now or never, he thought.
He flung open the empty locker and waved the empty envelope high.

"We did it!" he shouted, as if to a nearby companion. He
let out a loud, raucous laugh. "The Whipples fell for the
dummy key—we did it! We've got the Blues, baby. We're on
easy street now!"

As he'd expected, his jubilation didn't pass unnoticed.
People, taking him for a madman or a drunk, edged away

and he saw the three Whipples staring at him, exchanging stupefied glances that quickly turned to outrage.

With Gilbert in the lead, they stormed in his direction.

"No, no—" he cautioned. Backing up, he waved the envelope. "Original deal or nothing, Whipple," he called to Gilbert. "The ring for the stamps." He waved the envelope again, then darted through the crowd. He figured his shouting might have inspired someone to call security. If he got collared, it would be all over. He took off, heading for the departure section, knowing he would find what he wanted there.

Going just slowly enough for the Whipples to follow, he finally located what he needed, a postal box. It was less crowded where he was now, with passersby too self-absorbed to pay him any special attention. He glanced around for Tara, telling himself she was back in the other section and forcing himself not to worry about her. She'd shown she could take care of herself pretty damned well—she was some special kind of lady. Backing up against the postbox, he prepared himself for an onslaught of Whipples. They appeared on cue, the three of them still so steamed over the supposed dummy key that they hadn't thought to fan out. Confident in their number, they advanced on him like a slow, dangerous machine ready to mow him down.

When Sam judged that Gilbert was close enough for him to speak to him in almost a normal tone, he said, "Okay, Whipple," empty envelope held high in one hand, he extended his other hand palm up, fingers wiggling. "I get the ring, you get the stamps. It's that easy. Fool around and we attract too much attention, it's all over for all of us. Take the trade while you can or kiss the stamps goodbye." He poked the end of the envelope into the postal drop slot.

Gilbert blanched, stopping the advance. Eyes narrowed, he considered the situation.

"That's it," Sam encouraged. "The stamps are worth so much more and you know it. Too bad to have them disappear, courtesy of the U.S. Post Office. If we can deal, I'll set them on top of the box. I'll move away, you toss me the ring."

Sam watched as Gilbert slowly started to slip off the ring. He was making a blasted striptease out of it, Sam thought. Then he realized that the other two Whipples had regained their wits and were starting to spread out, intending to surround him. *Keep your cool, Sam,* he instructed himself. *Just keep your cool....*

"Come on," he coaxed, "toss it over." He saw that Gilbert had finished taking the ring off.

"On top of the box," Gilbert mouthed.

Forced into proving his willingness to play along, Sam tipped the envelope from the drop slot and held it as if ready to lay it on top of the box. Those clowns were going to rush him, he thought, unable to keep a watch on all three of them at once. Maybe, just maybe, he thought desperately, Gilbert would roll the ring along the floor to distract him, trusting that he would be able to grab it back when his flunkies moved in. But since he wouldn't be trying to protect the empty envelope, Sam would be free to concentrate on the Bonbon while the three crooks would be busy trying to grab everything—

The envelope was snatched from his hand.

"Ah, sh—" he began with a groan. Without the dummy envelope, everything was over. Either Elmo or Moss must have moved like lightning....

He looked around. *Tara?*

Tara held the envelope in her hand.

"Now hear this," she said, running back a few steps, flashing a warning glance at Moss, who was the closest to her. She had to raise her voice because a new influx of departure passengers was filing in, toting luggage and wearing buttons and funny hats.

She shifted her gaze to Gilbert, who still held the ruby ring in his hand. "Toss the ring to Sam, and I'll put down the envelope." Seeing that Elmo was trying to sneak up on her other side, she angled around, nearly bumping against a heavyset couple, part of a homeward-bound party who'd stopped to bid farewell to friends.

"Do as she says," Sam told Gilbert, never feeling more proud of her. "You can't get us both, and none of us can risk further commotion." He glanced over at Tara again. He saw she was putting the envelope down, tucking it through the handle of a suitcase. A blue suitcase . . .

With a curse, Gilbert rolled the ring across the floor. Sam dived for it at the same time as Moss dived for the envelope. Moss's fumbling hands landed on the blue suitcase.

"Lady!" Tara called out. "Watch your bag!"

"What?" The heavyset woman whirled in shock. "Horace—it's happening again! Some man is stealing our suitcase!" Screaming, she struck Moss with a furled umbrella.

Abandoning the ring, Gilbert, followed by Elmo, rushed over, either to save Moss or to grab the envelope, and by that time the woman's husband and her friends were shouting for security. The guards arrived and rushed into the fray.

Sam signaled to Tara, indicating a nearby escalator. They melted through a crowd being drawn by the ruckus and met by the moving stairs. They hopped aboard.

"Did you get the ring?" she asked, her eyes eager.

He flashed a grin and showed his hand. The Bonbon, winking warmly, sat securely on his little finger.

Riding up the stairs, they looked back. Two regular police officers had joined the security guards who'd nabbed the Whipples. They opened Gilbert's jacket, finding his gun. The escalator moved on. Tara's and Sam's last view of the scene below was Gilbert already in handcuffs and the other two Whipples being frisked.

"Handcuffs?" Tara questioned excitedly, as they stepped off at the top of the escalator. "To put them in handcuffs, the police must know who they are. Norman Nelson must have tipped off the police after all."

"No, I think it was the guns," Sam said. "Guns in an airport and all hell breaks loose." He chuckled. "The Whipples are in hot water now. When the police get them to the station it will come out that they already have a record." He chuckled again. "You've gotten your wish. They'll end up in jail, where they belong."

"And you're getting yours. You'll end up with the Dwight-Astor account. It all worked out, didn't it?"

Sam hugged her close as they walked along, leaving the congested section of the airport. He'd heard there were viewing decks in the airport, reached by a shuttle bus. Maybe they would go there, relax a little, unwind. It seemed petty to regret losing the Blues, but he couldn't seem to get them out of his head. How great it would have been to have had it all. What had happened to the locker key? He supposed the Whipples had ditched it. If the police found the key on them and opened the locker, the stolen stamps would only be one more nail in the gang's coffin. Don't get the blues over the Blues, he told himself. The Whipples were caught and he had the ring. He should be satisfied with that. And Tara. The very best part was Tara.

"You were absolutely terrific," he told her, giving her another hug. "When you took that envelope from my hand—*wow!*"

She laughed. "When you opened that locker and started yelling that you had the Blues—double *wow*."

"So you saw that?"

"What do you think? You should have known better than to tell me to stay out of the action."

"I guess I should have." Slowing his step, he drew her to a stop by a wide, sunny window. Leaning against the glass, he stood with his arms around her waist and gazed into her eyes. He was positive there wasn't a more beautiful pair of eyes in the entire world.

"I didn't want you hurt," he said, "but now I've been thinking—maybe we work better as a team."

"A similar thought has crossed my mind."

"Oh, it has?"

"It has. When you told Gilbert you were willing to give up the ring for me—" Her voice trembled with the emotions she felt when she remembered that moment. "I knew how much the ring meant to you. Being willing to give it up for me—that was really special."

"You're even more special."

"More special than prissy white gloves and the proper finger curled when drinking tea?"

"Much more than that. That's all part of you, but then there's the little girl playing Sheena of the Jungle who grew up to leap through bus windows and drive getaway cars and stop traffic in the most literal sense imaginable."

When he'd started talking there'd been a twinkle in his eyes, but by the time he was finished, his expression was serious. He ran his hands through her hair and lifted her face to his, kissing her tenderly. "It would have killed me if anything had happened to you," he whispered softly. He dropped his arms to her shoulders, pulling her against his body, then looking down into her face. "I wasn't being just a nice guy when I begged Gilbert to let you go. I'm in love with you, Tara. When I said I thought we'd make a good team, that's what I really meant.''

Smile radiant, Tara wrapped her arms around him. ''That's what I meant, too.''

He kissed her again, then laughed softly. ''I've just realized you're exactly what I thought you were at the beginning—a thief. And what you've stolen is my heart.''

They embraced again and then just stood holding each other close until the takeoff of a jumbo jet drew their attention. Turning toward the window, they stood arm in arm, watching the plane soar into the sky.

Sam's voice took on a sad note. ''I feel like that's a reminder that I'll soon have to be seeing about my return flight.''

Tara looked at him with dismay. ''You can't extend your time here?''

He thought of the hotel room and Tara, the Miami sun and sea and Tara. Then he sighed. ''Believe me, there's nothing I'd like better, but my company...''

She tilted her head, brushing a lock of hair back behind her ear. ''If they knew you'd made a smart move to save them money, mightn't they give you a few extra days to...settle things?''

He looked at her. ''You mean the ring? That was insured with us, but Freddy never reported it stolen, so there's no benefit to the company in getting it back. I only stand to win something because of Freddy's promise.''

She shook her head. ''I mean the Blues. Your outfit insured them, didn't they?''

''Sure, the stamps were insured for a bundle, so I guess I could have had a bonus if I'd gotten them, but if the Whipples have any brains at all, the key's gone for good, unless somebody finds it—'' He broke off, staring into her face, seeing the light in her eyes, hardly daring to hope.

"Tara? Don't tell me . . . you didn't . . ."

She shrugged. "You were shouting and waving the empty envelope and nobody was paying attention to me. Gilbert had already put the key in the locker and it seemed such a waste to leave the Blues sitting there where anyone could get them. So . . ." She shrugged again.

"We got them both?" He could hardly believe it. "The ring *and* the stamps?"

"Right here." Smiling, she opened her purse.

Sam stared at the stamps. "Tara, you're wonderful!" With an exhilarated laugh, he picked her up and swung her around. "You're the most wonderful woman in the world. My angel, my sweetheart, my princess, my—"

She stopped him, putting a finger to his lips. "I love you, Sam Miller," she said with mock sternness. "I'll be yours for the rest of your life if you'll have me, but there's one thing you have to promise."

He grinned up at her, loving the sparkle in her eyes, loving everything about her. "Absolutely anything. I promise. What is it?"

"Please, never call me Princess."

*   *   *   *   *

Silhouette Romance™

COMING NEXT MONTH

#688 FATHER CHRISTMAS—Mary Blayney
Daniel Marshall had never thought he could have it all: his
precious daughters *and* the woman who'd given them a mother's
love. But Annie VerHollan believed in Christmas miracles....

#689 DREAM AGAIN OF LOVE—Phyllis Halldorson
Mary Beth Warren had left her husband, Flynn, upon discovering
the truth behind their vows. Now that they had a second chance,
could she risk dreaming again of love?

#690 MAKE ROOM FOR NANNY—Carol Grace
Maggie Chisholm planned to faithfully abide by her nanny
handbook. But the moment she laid eyes on Garrett Townsend
she broke the golden rule—by falling in love with her boss!

#691 MAKESHIFT MARRIAGE—Janet Franklin
Practical Brad Williamson had proposed to Rachel Carson purely
for the sake of her orphaned niece and nephew. But how long
could Rachel conceal her longing for more than a
makeshift marriage?

#692 TEN DAYS IN PARADISE—Karen Leabo
Carrie Bishop arrived in St. Thomas seeking adventure and found
it while hunting for treasure with Jack Harrington. But she
never counted on the handsome loner being her most
priceless find....

#693 SWEET ADELINE—Sharon De Vita
Adeline Simpson had gone to Las Vegas to find her grandfather
and bring him back home. Could casino owner Mac Cole
convince lovely Addy that she was missing a lot more?

AVAILABLE THIS MONTH:

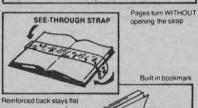

INDULGE A LITTLE SWEEPSTAKES
OFFICIAL RULES

SWEEPSTAKES RULES AND REGULATIONS. NO PURCHASE NECESSARY.

1. NO PURCHASE NECESSARY. To enter complete the official entry form and return with the invoice in the envelope provided. Or you may enter by printing your name, complete address and your daytime phone number on a 3 x 5 piece of paper. Include with your entry the hand printed words "Indulge A Little Sweepstakes." Mail your entry to: Indulge A Little Sweepstakes, P.O. Box 1397, Buffalo, NY 14269-1397. No mechanically reproduced entries accepted. Not responsible for late, lost, misdirected mail, or printing errors.

2. Three winners, one per month (Sept. 30, 1989, October 31, 1989 and November 30, 1989), will be selected in random drawings. All entries received prior to the drawing date will be eligible for that month's prize. This sweepstakes is under the supervision of MARDEN-KANE, INC. an independent judging organization whose decisions are final and binding. Winners will be notified by telephone and may be required to execute an affidavit of eligibility and release which must be returned within 14 days, or an alternate winner will be selected.

3. Prizes: 1st Grand Prize (1) a trip for two to Disneyworld in Orlando, Florida. Trip includes round trip air transportation, hotel accommodations for seven days and six nights, plus up to $700 expense money (ARV $3,500). 2nd Grand Prize (1) a seven-night Chandris Caribbean Cruise for two includes transportation from nearest major airport, accommodations, meals plus up to $1,000 in expense money (ARV $4,300). 3rd Grand Prize (1) a ten-day Hawaiian holiday for two includes round trip air transportation for two, hotel accommodations, sightseeing, plus up to $1,200 in spending money (ARV $7,700). All trips subject to availability and must be taken as outlined on the entry form.

4. Sweepstakes open to residents of the U.S. and Canada 18 years or older except employees and the families of Torstar Corp., its affiliates, subsidiaries and Marden-Kane, Inc. and all other agencies and persons connected with conducting this sweepstakes. All Federal, State and local laws and regulations apply. Void wherever prohibited or restricted by law. Taxes, if any are the sole responsibility of the prize winners. Canadian winners will be required to answer a skill testing question. Winners consent to the use of their name, photograph and/or likeness for publicity purposes without additional compensation.

5. For a list of prize winners, send a stamped, self-addressed envelope to Indulge A Little Sweepstakes Winners, P.O. Box 701, Sayreville, NJ 08871.

© 1989 HARLEQUIN ENTERPRISES LTD.

DL-SWPS

INDULGE A LITTLE SWEEPSTAKES
OFFICIAL RULES

SWEEPSTAKES RULES AND REGULATIONS. NO PURCHASE NECESSARY.

1. NO PURCHASE NECESSARY. To enter complete the official entry form and return with the invoice in the envelope provided. Or you may enter by printing your name, complete address and your daytime phone number on a 3 x 5 piece of paper. Include with your entry the hand printed words "Indulge A Little Sweepstakes." Mail your entry to: Indulge A Little Sweepstakes, P.O. Box 1397, Buffalo, NY 14269-1397. No mechanically reproduced entries accepted. Not responsible for late, lost, misdirected mail, or printing errors.

2. Three winners, one per month (Sept. 30, 1989, October 31, 1989 and November 30, 1989), will be selected in random drawings. All entries received prior to the drawing date will be eligible for that month's prize. This sweepstakes is under the supervision of MARDEN-KANE, INC. an independent judging organization whose decisions are final and binding. Winners will be notified by telephone and may be required to execute an affidavit of eligibility and release which must be returned within 14 days, or an alternate winner will be selected.

3. Prizes: 1st Grand Prize (1) a trip for two to Disneyworld in Orlando, Florida. Trip includes round trip air transportation, hotel accommodations for seven days and six nights, plus up to $700 expense money (ARV $3,500). 2nd Grand Prize (1) a seven-night Chandris Caribbean Cruise for two includes transportation from nearest major airport, accommodations, meals plus up to $1,000 in expense money (ARV $4,300). 3rd Grand Prize (1) a ten-day Hawaiian holiday for two includes round trip air transportation for two, hotel accommodations, sightseeing, plus up to $1,200 in spending money (ARV $7,700). All trips subject to availability and must be taken as outlined on the entry form.

4. Sweepstakes open to residents of the U.S. and Canada 18 years or older except employees and the families of Torstar Corp., its affiliates, subsidiaries and Marden-Kane, Inc. and all other agencies and persons connected with conducting this sweepstakes. All Federal, State and local laws and regulations apply. Void wherever prohibited or restricted by law. Taxes, if any are the sole responsibility of the prize winners. Canadian winners will be required to answer a skill testing question. Winners consent to the use of their name, photograph and/or likeness for publicity purposes without additional compensation.

5. For a list of prize winners, send a stamped, self-addressed envelope to Indulge A Little Sweepstakes Winners, P.O. Box 701, Sayreville, NJ 08871.

© 1989 HARLEQUIN ENTERPRISES LTD.

DL-SWPS

INDULGE A LITTLE—WIN A LOT!

Summer of '89 Subscribers-Only Sweepstakes

OFFICIAL ENTRY FORM

This entry must be received by: October 31, 1989
This month's winner will be notified by: Nov. 7, 1989
Trip must be taken between: Dec. 7, 1989–April 7, 1990
(depending on sailing schedule)

YES, I want to win the Caribbean cruise vacation for two! I understand the prize includes round-trip airfare, a one-week cruise including private cabin and all meals, and a daily allowance as revealed on the "Wallet" scratch-off card.

Name_____

Address_____

City_____ State/Prov._____ Zip/Postal Code_____

Daytime phone number_____
                                    Area code

Return entries with invoice in envelope provided. Each book in this shipment has two entry coupons — and the more coupons you enter, the better your chances of winning!
© 1989 HARLEQUIN ENTERPRISES LTD.

DINDL-2

INDULGE A LITTLE—WIN A LOT!

Summer of '89 Subscribers-Only Sweepstakes

OFFICIAL ENTRY FORM

This entry must be received by: October 31, 1989
This month's winner will be notified by: Nov. 7, 1989
Trip must be taken between: Dec. 7, 1989–April 7, 1990
(depending on sailing schedule)

YES, I want to win the Caribbean cruise vacation for two! I understand the prize includes round-trip airfare, a one-week cruise including private cabin and all meals, and a daily allowance as revealed on the "Wallet" scratch-off card.

Name_____

Address_____

City_____ State/Prov._____ Zip/Postal Code_____

Daytime phone number_____
                                    Area code

Return entries with invoice in envelope provided. Each book in this shipment has two entry coupons — and the more coupons you enter, the better your chances of winning!
© 1989 HARLEQUIN ENTERPRISES LTD.

DINDL-2